*U*ntil now I never thought twice about this painting. But as I carefully slip it out from behind the broken frame, avoiding the glass, I am surprised to discover a photograph behind it. I deftly slide this mysterious image out from its secret hiding place.

The picture is blurry, but from what I can make out from the dim light of the flashlight, it's a tall man wearing a dark raincoat with an old-time hat tilted over his forehead. It looks like a hat that an actor from a black-and-white movie might wear, the kind of old movie that they show on television in the middle of the night. If only the photographer (most likely Indigo) had remembered to use the focus button, I would be able to get a better sense of his features.

My heart speed races with each new thought that pops into my head until finally there's only one thought left: *I found him!* This is a photograph of Patch, my missing father!

Portia's Ultra Mysterious Double Life

ANNA HAYS

m!x
aladdin

ALADDIN MIX
NEW YORK   LONDON   TORONTO   SYDNEY

Children should always be supervised by an adult
when cooking and working in the kitchen.
The author and publisher expressly disclaim all responsibility
incurred as a consequence of the use and application
of any of the contents of this book.

ALADDIN MIX

Simon & Schuster Children's Publishing Division

1230 Avenue of the Americas, New York, NY 10020

Text copyright © 2008 by Anna Hays

All rights reserved, including the right of reproduction
in whole or in part in any form.

ALADDIN PAPERBACKS and related logo are registered trademarks
of Simon & Schuster, Inc.

ALADDIN MIX is a trademark of Simon & Schuster, Inc.

Designed by Karin Paprocki

The text of this book was set in Cochin.

Manufactured in the United States of America

First Aladdin Paperbacks edition March 2008

2 4 6 8 10 9 7 5 3 1

Library of Congress Control Number 2007932267

ISBN-13: 978-1-4169-4893-3

ISBN-10: 1-4169-4893-7

This book is dedicated to Susie, Elsa, and my mom, Sylvia.

ACKNOWLEDGMENTS

Thanks to Matt Saver, Dan Lazar, and Liesa Abrams, and to chef Mani Niall for creating Indigo's recipes (www.manistestkitchen.com).

To my family: Stevie, Hannah, Joey, Olivia, Sophie, Mary, John, Josie, the Whalens, and to my extended family too.

To my beloved brother-in-law Daniel McGowan Hays.

To Norman, for looking after me and Portia.

To Loretta, Frederick, and Penny.

To all of Portia's friends who supported her throughout this extraordinary journey.

And to the three men in my life—Buzz, Will, and Benjamin.

Portia's Ultra Mysterious Double Life

Chapter 1

3:47 A.M.,

MY BEDROOM, PALMVILLE

Sleeping lightly. Suddenly, the earth starts to move. My room hula-hoops left to right until I'm dizzy. Last night on the evening news, the weatherman with a really strange haircut predicted another beautiful day in Southern California. He was way wrong.

At this very moment my cat, Freddy Fred Frederick, is MIA. Yesterday he must have been telling me something when he ran in perfect circles and then played dead. He has a talent for predicting natural disasters. Why didn't I listen to him instead of the bad-haired guy on the news? I could have been more prepared.

FACT: Frederick is a long-bodied gray-and-white cat with stubby legs who is under the delusion that he is a dog. To live out this strange perception of himself, he does things like wagging his tail, howling at the moon, and chasing mail carriers. Even though he's totally macho and reminds me of an Old West cowboy with a long tail, he's super terrified of earthquakes.

As I crawl around on all fours searching for my furry and loyal companion, I try to calm Frederick's frazzled cat nerves. "Where are you, Freddy Fred Frederick? Don't be scared. Life is unpredictable. Once you get used to that fact, you won't have to hide so much."

Over the sounds of books hailing and glass cracking, I hear a familiar noise. But soon it's clear that it's not my treasured feline meowing to me. It's my mother, Indigo, calling my name from the next room. "Portia, are you okay?"

"Yes, Mom," I say, checking myself up and down. At least I think I'm okay.

Then the earth stops doing its crazy dance. There's an eerie silence for about three seconds. Time feels suspended, like in a movie. I look around my room and find myself

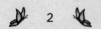

moving in slow motion. I don't recognize anythin[g] because nothing is where it's supposed to be. My b[ed is] on the floor, my desk is turned upside down, and my favorite and only cat is nowhere to be seen.

My nerves are on red alert. I've lived through earth-quakes before. Seven to be exact, but this one is different. This time when the floorboards shook left to right to an angry beat, the sound was so intense, I had to plug my ears. It was like going to the loudest rock concert ever, only there wasn't a stage or an audience. I was all by myself. This time I wasn't sure the earth was ever going to stop moving.

For one nanosecond I even imagined myself sailing over a rough sea, as though the floor were actually boards of a deck on a huge sailboat. Waves were splash-ing over me, again and again and again. But the smell of dust filling the air and the roar of fire trucks revving their engines within earshot of our home reminds me that I am in fact standing on the ground (that's not exactly level anymore), not stuck in the middle of the ocean dodging monster waves or fighting hard against seasickness.

I rush to where the mirror used to hang on the wall, but that's MIA too. I find my way to the bathroom and take a long look in the mirror (that's still there!). I see a seriously tired-looking twelve-year-old girl staring back at me. Just then a shadowy figure appears behind me. I scream at the top of my lungs. I *am* in a movie! And it's the kind I'm not allowed to see until I'm seventeen, unless accompanied by an adult.

Indigo squeezes me like a tube of toothpaste that's just about to run out. "My sweet Portia!"

OBSERVATION: Moms tend to get really dramatic about missing children and earthquakes.

Running my hands over my body from head to toe, I answer her. "I'm fine, Indigo, but I can't find Frederick. He bolted from under the covers as soon as the shaking began, and now he's missing."

"We'll find him. He couldn't have gone too far."

Indigo hands me a really ancient flashlight. Together we search for Frederick. As I squirm under the bed, I spot the oval green eyes of my cat staring back at me. When I

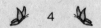

call his name, he responds with a shaky meow. It's going to take the whole Palmville Hook and Ladder Company No. 1 to pull him out from this hiding spot. At least I know he's safe. And it's unlikely that he'll be changing his newly discovered secure position anytime soon.

Indigo suggests we check out the rest of the damage to the house. I volunteer for the upstairs while she takes the downstairs. She already has a broom ready for me. This is not the kind of broom that would be advertised at your local hardware store. It's a witch's dream broom. I say this because it appears to have been created in the middle of the woods by crafty forest dwellers. I take hold of the oversized stick that still has bark on it and sweep a path across the hallway toward Indigo's bedroom, leaving heaps of plaster dust on either side of me.

From downstairs, I hear Indigo call up to me, "Portia, how does it look?"

Coughing from a new cloud of dust that has just surfaced, I swipe at the air, trying to get a clear view of the damage. Something catches my eye, and I make my way toward it. "Still figuring that out, Mom."

"Be careful, sweetheart. You are wearing your slippers, aren't you?"

I look down at my bare feet on the worn Persian rug. "Uh-huh."

> **FACT:** Indigo Avatar is a single, bohemian earth mother who tries really hard to make me feel safe and secure. She thinks about my happiness every waking day. And she's got the most positive attitude in the entire galaxy. The only time I see her lose her chamomile state of calm is when I ask her about my missing father, Patch.

My father, Patch, is on a fantastic voyage. I know this because I receive scented postcards from exotic places around the world, and they are signed by him. I should say that these postcards appear to me in my dreams, in Technicolor. Patch is the most mysterious and elusive detective to ever hit planet Earth. I have deduced that the only reason he's not here in Palmville with his daughter, wife, and gray-and-white scaredy-cat is because he is undercover somewhere solving the insolvable and saving lives and/or maybe even entire countries.

For some reason (yet to be determined), my mother is very vague about my traveling father. I try my best to talk to her about this very sensitive (and important!) issue, but she avoids the subject, insisting that when I turn sixteen, she will sit me down and tell me everything she knows about him. Doesn't she have even a fraction of a clue that I am twelve going on one hundred and five, and I am more than ready to hear the truth about my missing father?

The unsolved mystery of my father's whereabouts always sets off a funny feeling in my stomach. It's times like this one, when life brings me a totally unexpected surprise (and I'm not talking about a birthday party or a fortune cookie), that I miss Patch most. If he were here with us in Palmville right now, I know for a fact that he would either be checking the gas line just outside our house or securing the perimeter to ensure that Indigo and I (and Frederick) are safe from exposed electrical wires, broken glass, and other post-earthquake hazards.

I tread carefully around the room inspecting the damage and spot a small picture frame covered with shattered glass. I sweep the stray shards of glass away, then kneel down to take a closer look. The painting is of an unfamiliar landscape that looks like it's far, far away from Palmville. It's been hanging on the wall in my mom's room since I was a baby. Until now I never thought twice about it. But as I carefully slip it out from behind the broken frame, avoiding the glass, I am surprised to discover a photograph behind it. I deftly slide this mysterious image out from its secret hiding place.

The picture is blurry, but from what I can make out from the dim light of the flashlight, it's a tall man wearing a dark raincoat with an old-time hat tilted over his forehead. It looks like a hat that an actor from a black-and-white movie might wear, the kind of old movie that they show on television in the middle of the night. If only the photographer (most likely Indigo) had remembered to use the focus button, I would be able to get a better sense of his features.

My heart speed races with each new thought that pops into my head until finally there's only one thought left: *I found him!* This is a photograph of Patch, my missing father!

The earth isn't moving now, but I feel the floor slip out from under me. If this is truly a picture of Patch, I have stumbled upon the most important photograph of my entire existence to date. I know there is something I should be doing at this moment, something significant. But I can't exactly shout with joy and leap into the air with "I've just landed on Jupiter" excitement. I've got to keep this important finding a total secret or Indigo will freak out. I close my eyes to double-check that this is in fact not a dream. I slowly count to ten. Quietly, I begin: "One, two, three . . ."

When I get to "three," I hear the wind chimes ring from downstairs. That's Indigo calling me to join her in the kitchen. She shouts up to me, "You're so quiet up there! Is everything all right?"

It's obvious that I am not dreaming now, which sends my heart soaring high over the dusty mountains of Palmville. I open my eyes and want to shout, *Yes, now that I have found the first material evidence of my long-lost father after twelve years of wondering, dreaming, hoping, and longing, everything is extremely fine. Now that I have a major clue to Patch's identity and my life is about to change forever,*

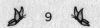

everything is totally amazing, but instead, I keep this life-altering secret hidden in my back pocket and respond calmly, devoid of any emotion, pretending to be a robot. "It's totally normal up here, Mom. I'll be right down."

Chapter 2

I rush to my bedroom to hide the picture of Patch. I search for the biggest book left on my painted pink polka-dotted bookshelf that isn't buried under a pile on the floor. It's *The Absolute Complete Unabridged Version of the History of the World*. That book hasn't been opened for maybe three hundred years and probably won't be opened for a hundred more. The mysterious photo will be safe there for sure.

Then I find my furry tiger slippers and check on Frederick, who is still in the same terrified cat position under the bed. Leaning over to try to spot him, I offer some words of wisdom. "Frederick, fear is just a temporary state. Soon hunger will set in, and all you'll be thinking about is food."

As I sit on the side of my messy bed slipping my rough-soled feet into my soft slippers, I notice that the red message light on my effervescent pink PDA is blinking. It still works! I find it semi-comforting to know that the world hasn't entirely stopped just because of the morning's seismic shaking.

Before discovering the photo of my dad, my PDA (aka personal digital assistant) was my most precious material object. It's where I keep all the thoughts and secrets that rush through my head each day and every night while I sleep. This treasured electronic device also works as a phone. After much begging and pleading, Indigo finally bought me one for safety reasons. In case, for instance, I'm stranded in the middle of nowhere and need to communicate with someone like her. Or if there's an emergency like an earthquake or some other unnaturally harsh natural disaster.

I quickly check the message on my PDA. It's from Amy Clamdigger, my best friend since kindergarten.

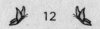

12

P, can you believe we just had an 8.1! >:-C

Did you survive? B4N, Amy

FACT: Even though Amy C sometimes has a habit of getting on my nerves, she does truly care about my mental and physical well-being.

IDENTIFYING DATA

SUBJECT: Amy Clamdigger (aka the Clamdigger, the Amester, Ame). Red hair. Blue eyes. Twelve years old. Puddles of freckles. Boy crazy. Loves to outdo friends in everything (e.g., in school, romance, fashion). Is known to be fun and entertaining but can be annoying at times.

NATURE OF CONTACT: Friend and confidant.

LENGTH OF CONTACT: Ever since the first day of kindergarten.

BACKGROUND MATERIAL: Subject lives with her family of five siblings and two busy parents in the house down the street. Has a long history of bragging about herself. Despite that, she has always proven to be a good friend.

The wind chimes ring again. They're louder this time. I shout downstairs, "Coming, Indigo!"

I quickly respond to the Amester, telling her that, in fact, I survived and that something groundbreaking has happened to me, and it's very personal so please be super closedmouthed about it. Just after I send my message, the phone fizzles out. It must be because of the quake. No electricity and now the phones are dead!

I look down at my hands. They're shaking! I clasp them together and squeeze them, whispering to myself, "This is not a dream, Portia. You're awake." I stare at the far corner of my room to see how long I can keep staring without blinking.

My spell is broken by the wind chimes again and the insistent, singsong voice of my mom. "Portia, what are you doing up there? Come on downstairs!"

As I head down the rickety wooden stairs to the kitchen, a piece of the wall hits the floor. The house is crying plaster tears. I open my eyes wider and now see cracks in the walls everywhere. Little slits lead to a jagged path to an even bigger opening, bigger than any Band-Aid could ever possibly cover.

FACT: Indigo, Frederick, and I live in a hundred-year-old California bungalow. The outside of our house is painted white, just like Dorothy's house in THE WIZARD OF OZ. There are lemon, lime, and orange trees in the backyard. The smell of fresh lavender seeps through the cracks in the windowsills. In the front yard there's a giant fig tree with leaves that look like extra-large gloves. Our house is surrounded by a funky old wooden fence that is frozen Tin Man–like in this lopsided position. Just outside the front gate that never quite closes, balancing on a slanted wooden post, stands an oversized mailbox with a miniature door that never quite closes either. Come to think of it, as I run through my house touching every corner with my mind, I don't find a single right angle in the whole place. Are right angles reserved for geometry class, or do they really exist?

Usually, the inside of my house is a festival of color, smell, and texture. The aromas of basil, lemon, sage, and patchouli fill the air. An international mix of rugs from Persia and India and Mexico covers the hardwood floors. One entire living room wall is filled with books, in shelves that provide a quiet home for literature from past centuries. There are self-help books, NATIONAL GEOGRAPHIC collections with photographs of people and landscapes from around the world, and small handmade paperbacks full of homegrown poetry. In the kitchen shiny copper pots and pans line the walls and hang from the ceiling.

Now, as I make my way down the stairs, I can see the effect of that crazy dance performed by the angry gods from the heavens. The brick chimney has crumbled down into our already cluttered living room, and our floor is caked with soot and random pieces of red brick. Books are spread out all over the rug. Our indoor plants have spilled their rich soil, exposing the roots of the jungle-size leafy trees my mom has been nurturing for a trillion years.

Just before I enter the kitchen, I look out of the hall window and wonder how the other Palmville families are handling this early-morning surprise. What earth-shattering occurrences are they experiencing at this very moment?

4:12 A.M.,

AVATAR KITCHEN

In the kitchen I discover that Indigo has miraculously prepared a way-too-early-in-the-morning post-earthquake snack. As she sweeps up the broken pieces of our handmade clay dishes that cover the tiled floor, she insists that everything is going to get back to normal. I look at the plate of organic garbanzo beans, lentils, and tahini and know in my heart that even though the vegetarian cuisine looks familiar, things in the Avatar home are never going to be quite the same. I slowly consume the healthy treats, careful not to drop any clues about my new discovery.

Indigo is the sole proprietor of a health food restaurant located in downtown Palmville called Contentment (aka The Tent). She, along with her chef-in-training, Hap Lester, manages to take natural, organic ingredients and create delicacies from them (some of them aren't as delectable as others, I have to admit). While most kids eat breakfasts that consist of Lucky Charms, Cocoa Puffs, and Pop-Tarts, I am Indigo's guinea pig, tasting and testing recipes for The Tent's always changing menu. On a typical morning I might end up eating a bowl of beans, for example, as my first meal of the day. Beans! Of course, you wouldn't know they're beans at first glance. Indigo is a genius at the camouflage of beans. She can make bean breakfast cereal, bean pudding, bean pie, bean spaghetti, and red and black bean baked Alaska without anyone knowing that these treats are actually made of beans.

Sometimes I feel like I just can't deal with this menu-testing stuff, but on this occasion, as I dip into the pile of garbanzo beans (that are not disguised as anything but themselves), I pretend to be thrilled with the nutritive value of the most widely consumed legume in the world. This is definitely not the right moment to express my innermost true feelings about my mom's radically sugar-free, all-natural recipes. I know how much time and care she puts into preparing her nourishing meals. I wouldn't want to upset her with my less-than-gentle opinion of her cooking. Frankly, I would rather crunch on tasteless beige beans than raise even the slightest suspicion from my unsuspecting vegetarian mother.

I look over at Indigo, who is busy pouring the remnants of our dinner plates into a recycled garbage bag, when she turns to me and smiles. How does she do it? I mean, she's smiling in the face of this ridiculously uncertain time. Who knows when an aftershock will hit? Her nerves must be made of titanium. Maybe there's something I can learn from her. If I did ever learn the secret of how she stays so inexplicably serene, the very first thing I'd do is rush to tell Frederick, who is still probably frozen in his "I'm so entirely terrified of earthquakes" pose.

I look at the clock: 4:23 a.m. In approximately three hours I have to wake up again to go to Palmville Middle School, and I haven't even gone to sleep yet. Suddenly, school seems very far away. How can I possibly care about pop quizzes, bad hair days, and beauty makeovers now that I've found a major clue to the true identity of my missing father? How can math homework ever have any meaning again? Calculating the perimeter of a parallelogram really doesn't make sense to me now that a piece of my family history is about to be revealed.

Indigo catches me lost in my thoughts. Ever the observant mother, she looks me up and down, sensing something is different about me. I freeze, holding a spoonful of tahini in my hand while it slowly oozes onto one of the few surviving salad plates. I silently ask the heavens above, *Please don't let Indigo notice that I am keeping a radical secret from her. From this point on, no matter what mood I'm in, I promise to be kind, considerate, and make the world a much better place than it was when I first got here.*

The clouds open up (the gods must have been listening) because Indigo turns to me and says softly, "You

 19

look tired, honey. It's time to go back to bed."

I stick the tahini into my mouth to mask my smile at the relief that she is so entirely clueless. The sticky, gooey paste makes it difficult to speak. I try to open my mouth but get only halfway there. I somehow manage to utter, "Awesome idea, Mom."

Chapter 3

A swarm of golden butterflies flutters past my window. I tear the covers off me and run toward the window hoping to catch a view of them, but all I see is a golden cloud way up high in the sky, disappearing before my eyes like the end of some mystical magic act. Presto! My room is back to its regular pre-earthquake "normal" state. Even Frederick is back, balled up in a circle at the bottom right corner of my bed (his favorite spot). I tiptoe downstairs, careful not to wake Indigo. Then I unlock the front door and step outside.

Wet dew seeps between my toes as I trek to the rusty old mailbox that sits precariously at the edge of our front yard. I open the miniature door that is barely hanging on to its hinges. Buried deep underneath the colorful piece of junk mail and the electric bill, I see an exotic-looking postcard. I can smell its rich aroma, a combination of nutmeg, cinnamon, and clove. It's from my father! A stray butterfly struggles to join his other friends, but his fragile right wing is stuck under a bright yellow YOU HAVE WON A MILLION DOLLARS sweepstakes envelope. I do my best to clear the way for him, and off he goes out of the mailbox, heading straight for the crescent moon high above our slanted roof.

My hands tremble as I reach for the postcard. The card has clearly traveled through deserts, floods, and crowded aircraft. And here it is in my hands, waiting to greet me on my own front lawn. The painted image on the front is of a ship sailing the high seas. A wave splashes the bow as brawny sailors work together to over-power the furious waters challenging them to a duel. Even though the ship is most likely a thousand miles away, it feels close to me, like one of those big sailboats docked at the marina down the coast. I squint my eyes like a wildlife photographer trying to focus on her prized subject. One of the sailors stands out from the rest. He's got a movie-star tan and is taller than the others. I turn the card over to read the message.

Patch has written something in purple ink, which has been smeared (maybe by one of the storms this magical postcard endured during its travels). The words are now abstract images that look like those psychological inkblot tests kids take when they have anger issues.

I breathe deeply and try to decipher the message. I hear myself breathing, louder and louder and deeper and deeper, until the sound of my own breath wakes me up. *DREAM ENDS.*

SECONDS LATER,
MY BEDROOM

I look up to find Indigo standing over my bed.

OBSERVATION: Indigo is dressed in a peasant blouse, drawstring pants, comfortable sandals, and beaded earrings. Her long, flowing brown hair is pulled back. She wears a purple crystal phoenix with long feathers around her neck and a concerned expression on her face.

My black-and-white striped kitty alarm clock reads 9:26 a.m. Bolting up, I quickly check out my room. It's still a mess from the earthquake. That's when I know for sure that I'm not dreaming anymore.

Panicked, I cry, "I'm late! Miss Killjoy does not tolerate tardiness! Why didn't you wake me? My flawless attendance record is now tragically in jeopardy."

"I tried. You were out cold. Besides, I thought I'd give you a little extra dream time since school is closed today."

"Seriously?" It's starting to sink in that life is most certainly going to be different from now on.

"School will be closed along with most of the businesses in town until Monday."

"That's huge!"

"The earthquake has affected the whole town, sweetheart. There's going to be a lot of work ahead for all of us."

"Is Frederick . . . ?"

"He's right here under the bed. I left him his favorite Barley Delight, so he'll be fine."

I think to myself that Frederick despises Indigo's home-cooked Barley Delights, so translated that means he's probably starving right about now. "Mom, barley isn't exactly Frederick's dream meal."

"Frederick loves my Barley Delights. Every time I make them for him, they're gone in a day."

"Have you ever actually seen him eat one?"

The wheels slowly start spinning inside Indigo's head. Before she connects the dots that lead to the super-obvious truth that Barley Delights are less than delicious, I cleverly (at least I think so) use the tried-and-true magician's trick of misdirection, reminding myself to act cucumber cool and not to stir the rice pot. Concerned that Indigo might be taking the news about the Barley Delights a bit too personally, I quickly change the subject to avoid even a minor tremor. "Mom, animals know things. They have extrasensory perception and can forecast future events like rainstorms, earthquakes, and the Fourth of July. Frederick tried to warn me about what was going to happen, but I didn't listen to him. Now I've got no other choice than to interpret his hiding under the bed to signify that the worst is not over. He's telling us that there will be more rumbling ahead."

 25

Indigo looks at me, wearing a crinkly concerned-mother face, worried about her only daughter's welfare. "Now, Portia, try to see this whole situation as an opportunity. When one of life's surprises turns up, there's a good chance you'll learn something new because of it."

I know that I am about to learn something new about my long-lost father, and so I reply to Indigo's "you're going to be all right, life has its challenges" speech with simply, "Right, Mom."

Indigo sees that I am not exactly myself, so she tries to help me feel better by making this dramatic situation of earthquake destruction all around us seem as normal as wheat-free vegan cinnamon buns with vanilla soy icing by switching to her dream-checking mode. "Well, did you have any dreams last night?"

DREAM CHECKER ALERT! Dream checking is a morning ritual in our household. It can be quite irritating, but I must indulge Indigo at least a couple of times a week. Even though our house is turned upside down and Palmville is in shambles, Indigo still wants to know about my dreams. She's so unbelievably dream crazy. She has this elephant-size theory

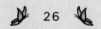

about how dreams are really guides, filled with symbols and signs that give us clues about ourselves. She insists that we should pay more attention to them. I bet if she wrote her theory down in longhand, it would reach from here to the top of the tallest palm tree in town and back again.

I avoid direct eye contact with her when I say, "I dreamed about him last night."

Indigo's body stiffens like she's just seen a ghost. Then, cleverly deflecting, she responds, "Who?"

Smiling, I tell her, "Patch."

Making a complete U-turn in our conversation (is that legal?), she looks around my room and says calmly, "I think it's time we started to clean up this mess."

I catch myself wondering why she can't just be straightforward with her inquisitive twelve-year-old only daughter. That's when I wisely put on the brakes and make an abrupt stop. I decide not to push for a clue about the mystery of my missing father this time, cautious not to reveal anything about my discovery last night. Instead, I play it like a jazz saxophone player. Real smooth. "You're absolutely right, Mom. Definitely."

She squints at me like she's the wildlife photographer now, zeroing in on her subject. I'm 99 percent sure she was expecting me to ask about Patch's identity and whereabouts like I do every time the subject arises, but I refuse to give her even half a millisecond to question my sincerity and catch on that there are big changes stirring inside about to surface. I cover up by quickly adding in a sugary sweet tone, "I'm so entirely happy that we all survived the quake! Earthquakes bring families together, don't they?"

Still squinting at her subject (me!), she says softly, "They certainly do."

Chapter 4

Indigo is downstairs cleaning up and preparing breakfast. I'm supposed to be assessing the damage in my room, but my mind drifts to my new discovery. The thought that I might be getting closer to my father is superglued to my brain. I crawl through tossed and spilled objects that cover my purple zebra-striped throw rug and take out the extra-large *History of the World* book that contains the photo of him. As I study the faded and torn image, I can definitely tell that this man is a great detective. The hat. The raincoat. The mysterious expression on his face. And his sly sidelong glance. Patch is truly a man of many hats and disguises.

Then I have a mind-stretching revelation. Here it is: I too have the qualities of a detective. I have been a curious person since my first day on Earth. Ever since I can remember, I find myself seeing things about people that other people can't see. Did you know that there is hidden meaning in everything a person says and does?

My PDA is loaded with personal data, observations, and notes about friends, teachers, Frederick, and my mom. Sometimes I even make notes about people I barely know, like the mailman who wears a folded red handkerchief in his back pocket and is terrified of dogs or the guy who sells ice cream and never smiles even though he's got the sweetest job in town. I carry this digital notebook with me as a way to capture what I think is going on inside my various subjects' minds and what I know is going on inside mine. Every day I try to catch the facts, the thoughts, and the moments as they happen, so my trusty PDA is always within arm's reach.

Of course! I've inherited my father's detective genes!

Destiny is a force that sweeps you up, like the unpredictable twister that lifted Dorothy and her dog and all her furniture and flew them across the sky to Oz. Sometimes there's a rainbow on the other side, but sometimes there's just another mysterious universe that needs exploration, almost like the one you just left, only with more at stake.

It is clear what I must do now. Destiny has speed-dialed me, and I am picking up the phone. As of today, Thursday morning at 9:57 a.m. in the sleepy, tropical town of Palmville (my home), I am officially *Portia Avatar: Girl Psychoanalytic Detective*. Still wearing my pj's, I scramble through the heap of clothes that used to be hanging in my closet. Miraculously, I find my trusty magenta knitted cap. When I place it on my unwashed hair, I feel like myself for the first time in about six hours. I adjust it on my head, ensuring that its angle is just right. Then I apply my treasured cherry pop lip gloss, which I have managed to recover from the massive junk pile formerly known as my bedroom floor.

I'm ready for my first case, which has presented itself. If this were a movie, the sound effect right now would be a thunderbolt striking loudly followed by an overly dramatic pause. But since it's real life, the only

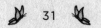

sound track I hear is the hum of a helicopter in the distance and another fire truck turning the corner, reminders that our humble abode is not the only place that has been affected by Mother Nature's most recent freak-out.

My first and most groundbreaking case will be called "The Case of Patch, My Missing Father: A Man of Many Hats." It will undoubtedly prove to be the most challenging one of my career. Even though my career is only a few minutes old, I feel this is in my heart, which is beating extra fast at the moment.

IMPORTANT NOTE: The reason that my dad is a man of many hats is because he is the ultimate traveler. Since he wears a total detective chapeau in the picture I found of him, I believe that in his travels he must wear a variety of disguises that incorporate different hats. A beret in France, a fez in Morocco, a panama hat in Panama, and a top hat in England. He probably carries an entire suitcase just for his hats!

A good detective knows how to pace herself, and that's what I plan to do. My new life as a detective will

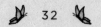

remain a secret. Not a soul must know about my ultra mysterious double life.

I reach for my PDA again to try to make contact with Miss Clamdigger (aka Amy) to tell her all about it. Amazingly, my treasured electronic device works this time. How random!

I quickly text her the news:

> 8-] Ame. I have a new career. I'm a detective. VBG. I plan on solving the mysteries of people and their perplexing human behavior. I'm not motivated by fame or fortune. My number one career goal is to find my long-lost father, then pursue cases in and around Palmville. Isn't that cool? B4N. Portia. P.S. Do you notice that cherry pop lip gloss totally comes in handy after an earthquake? Speaking of lips, please keep yours sealed. :-# My mission is potentially life changing, and I can't risk any foul play. TU!

Suddenly, Indigo's organic Barley Delight (that's not so delightful) spins across the floor like a flying saucer in its final stages of descending to Earth. Frederick is telling me something. He must be bored. Or maybe he's desperate for real food. He mustn't starve. I don't know what I'd do without him.

Crawling jungle-marine-style under the bed, I whisper to him, "Barley is gnarly, I know. I appreciate the reminder, Frederick. I'm totally on the case." Heroically, with a sense of calm command, I utter, "Wait right there"—like he's really going to move—"I've got it under control."

He meows at me, as if to say, *Thanks, Sergeant. I'll cover the bedroom while you seek out the grub.*

I quickly change into daylight clothes. My favorite olive green corduroy hip-huggers are not where I left them yesterday. Presumably, they're in some opposite corner of the room, buried somewhere under this earthquake-induced chaos. At least I've got my hat! I grab whatever clothes I can find that are halfway decent. As I put on my third-favorite pair of embroidered jeans and desperately look for a top to match, it's starting to hit me that life has become so supremely hectic. For example, my cat is hungry right now, and I'm not sure I'll be able to find his favorite cat food for him. There's a good chance the stores will be closed for days, which means a possible full week-end of my lovable, furry object of affection avoiding Barley Delights. Just then another treat comes flying out from under the bed, skating across the floor. An even louder meow follows.

"Frederick, I've got your best interest in mind. It's just that sometimes there are things you can't exactly control. I know this is hard to hear, but I can't guarantee I'll be able to find our secret stash of Fancy Feast chicken nibblets. Nothing is exactly normal at the moment."

It's not even noon, and yesterday seems like at least two hundred and fifty years ago. I look around my messy room that's radically more messy since the quake, and I notice that some of my favorite material possessions have broken: my heart-shaped jewelry box and a collection of colorful bottles that used to line my windowsill. What strikes me most is that I don't care that they are ruined and lost forever. Maybe that's because I know what's important in my life now. Since finding the hidden photo of Patch, I have seriously rearranged my priorities.

I hear a gravelly meow from under the bed. "Okay, okay. I'm on my way to the kitchen. It's just that I'm trying to get my priorities straight, and also, I can't seem to find my favorite aquamarine pleather belt."

Chapter 5

*D*ownstairs, I check the kitchen's painted gold cabinets for any sign of surviving cat food. The doorbell rings (at least that still works), followed by a series of furious knocks.

Indigo has just walked in from the backyard carrying one of her assortment of oversized hemp bags. This one is filled with bright yellow lemons and deep green limes picked from our fruit trees out back. She hurriedly pours the fruit into a wobbly, handmade clay bowl and rushes with curiosity to the door.

It's Hap, who has come over to report on The Tent.

NOTE: Hap Lester, my mom's chef-in-training. He graduated from college a few years ago. Now he's in graduate school doing a cross-cultural study of love rituals. On Wednesday nights he performs spoken word at the Cappuccino Café. Hap has a gigabyte crush on Indigo, who doesn't notice his warm smile and serious eyes.

QUESTIONS: Isn't "love" supposed to be simple, like the wind or riding a bicycle downhill? How could something as obvious as a major crush go so completely unnoticed? Could it be that Indigo is aware of Hap's intense feelings for her and only pretends to be in the dark?

Usually, Hap finds every excuse in the universe to come over to our house off-hours to spend "quality time" with Indigo. For example, "Indigo, you left your umbrella at the restaurant, and the rainy season is only thirty-four weeks away." Or "Thanksgiving is in eight months, so I thought you might want to hear about a new sweet potato recipe I dreamed up last night." And sometimes it's "I was just in the neighborhood and noticed the lights were on." Isn't he aware that Indigo has his address and knows for certain that he lives way on the other side of town?

However, on this particular visit Hap has a totally legit reason for knocking on the door. I try to listen in on his conversation with Indigo, but their flourish of whispers blurs, making one utterance indecipherable from the next. Then Indigo, who's usually so inexplicably mellow, shrieks loudly. The shrieking adds a new layer of tension to the room. She shouts my name and grabs another one of her oversized hemp bags from the collection. "We have to get to The Tent, *now*!"

I look down at my hands. They're trembling again. I try to shake them out, but my nerves have officially taken over. Just then the floorboards start to squeak and whine. I quickly race under a doorframe and hold on as tightly as I can while Indigo and Hap crawl under the kitchen table.

It's an aftershock!

Once we all sense that it's over and not going to turn into something bigger, like another quake, we slowly revert to our pre-aftershock positions, this time a little more alert and a lot more on edge.

 39

Indigo is very insistent. "We've got to go right now, P."

But right now I can think about only one thing. "Frederick! I can't leave him alone. He'll starve."

Indigo throws a few more random items into her hemp bag. Then she looks over and assures me, "He's got the Barley Delights. Those will keep him nourished until we get back."

Since Indigo refuses to accept that Frederick's kitty taste buds have zero interest in barley anything, I decide that arguing with her now would only upset her and possibly compromise the case. So I swallow the truth and mumble to myself, "Exactly, he'll starve!"

To Indigo, I say, "I'm pretty sure I left something in the kitchen."

I slip away, knowing that I must act quickly (and discreetly). After all, my only cat's mental, physical, and emotional health is at stake. Not to mention his extreme state of hunger. I take two bowls from the kitchen cabinet that miraculously survived the shaking and fill one with water. In the other I put a scoop from the secret stash of Fancy Feast chicken nibblets (I found it!).

I slide the kitty cat banquet under the bed. I lean my head down and whisper, "There's trouble with Contentment. I've got to help Indigo. She's totally freaking out, and my hunch (and fear) is that this might just be the beginning of a long list of unexpected discoveries today. I love you, Frederick! I promise I'll be back soon. And don't worry. There will be no more barley in your future if I have anything to do with it."

10:29 A.M.,

OUTSIDE AVATAR HOME

I ndigo and I climb into our first-generation hybrid. I carry my knapsack, which has my PDA tucked in the side pocket. Even though I'm not sure if I can connect to the outside world, I still have inner thoughts that must have a home. As long as the batteries work, my case notes can be recorded.

But I have to save my batteries now, so I make a mental note of Indigo's freak-out performance since Hap delivered news to her about The Tent. I'm really starting to wonder what he told her. I'm guessing I'll find out in about five and a half minutes. That's approximately the time it takes to get from our house to The Tent by car.

Hap follows closely behind us in his vintage convertible green Beetle, complete with scrapes and bruises that happen to all of us over time, especially when we're cars. I turn around and watch Hap as he looks at Indigo. He gets so entirely dreamy-eyed whenever he sees her. I hope he'll be able to stay focused on the road.

FACT: Hap Lester is the most romantic man in Palmville. He truly believes that he's destined to be with Indigo, and so he waits patiently, trusting in destiny, chopping carrots, parsley, and cabbage, cleaning sticky counters, and grating soy cheese at her restaurant. He is convinced that one golden California day Indigo will turn to him and accept his undying love with open arms.

Driving through town, my questions about how my neighbors fared after the quake are slowly being answered. Overturned lawn ornaments, broken windows, tilted carports, a few uprooted foundations.

Nobody seems to notice us pass by. I see the Chronicles, whose house is now leaning entirely to the right. I open the window to wave to them, but they don't see me. Mr. Chronicle is in the process of crawling under what's left of his front porch, while Mrs. Chronicle shakes her hands at him like a television actress who overacts while trying to make a point. My guess is that her point is maybe Mr. Chronicle should leave the dangerous under-the-porch work to the professionals. But his ears are deaf to her soap opera pleas. The earthquake has brought out his heroic side, and there's no stopping him.

Then I see Buzzie, the Chronicles' dog, down the street, running away from home at top speed. He's got a mad stare in his eyes, and his little terrier feet are blurry from the excessive speed of his run. Wilson Chronicle, the oldest boy in the trio of Chronicle kids, chases after him, wearing only his pj's. It's clear that the earthquake has shaken up the Chronicle family's equilibrium.

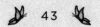

As our car slowly passes by, I shout to Wilson, "Is everything all right?"

He looks at me without uttering a sound. He's creepily silent. Then he just screams, "Buzzie!"

Usually when we drive to The Tent, it's "Good morning, Ms. and Miss Avatar, what's cooking at The Tent?" or "Hello, Indigo. Hello, Portia. Can you beat this weather?" But this morning small talk seems to be way too small.

I turn my attention to Indigo, who is at the wheel, determined to get to her destination. Her hands are white-knuckled, steering a direct course to her beloved place of business she built up from scratch. Contentment was created with love, care, and just the right ingredients, kind of like one of her homemade certified organic banana nut bars. One of the few desserts at The Tent that doesn't taste healthy!

My head is consumed with thoughts about my case. This trip to The Tent was not part of my strategy, but like any super-qualified detective, I have to flow with the situation. I risk battery time to make a note of this in my treasured PDA.

REMINDER: Until the electricity is back on, I'll refrain from overdoing the note-taking thing, even though it's one of the essentials of detective work. Instead, I'll take virtual snapshots of the world around me and file them in my brain.

We approach the center of town, nearing The Tent. I look through the picture windows of the local stores and see that the storeowners and their workers all seem to be scratching their heads, pondering what to do next. One of the shopkeepers from Hansel's Hardware waves at me. I wave back, relieved to know that there's at least one person out there who's acting quasi-normal. Then I notice she's actually pointing to a giant hole in the concrete road that Indigo just barely misses. Things really aren't quite the same in Palmville. That's for sure.

We turn the corner past the yogurt shop, Twist and Shout, with a big wooden board that usually posts the flavor of the day, like Peanut Butter Dream or Rainbow Delusion, but today it reads CLOSED UNTIL FURTHER NOTICE. I try to make peace with my current situation by convincing myself that spending the day on cleanup patrol at The Tent with Indigo gives me the opportunity of more alone time with her. Perhaps she'll offer me a clue to Patch's whereabouts. Maybe she'll even lead me to more material evidence.

My plan right now is to watch, listen, and process.

We continue on our way as I slip into a daydream. Leaning out the window, I think about my small tropical town that borders a big blue ocean filled with dark mysteries. In Palmville we live in an endless summer of cloudless days and starry nights. It's October, but the leaves don't really change here, not like in other places in the world. So if, for instance, it were May or July, it would basically look the same. The fall does bring cleaner air and slightly cooler nights. Otherwise, it's the same tropical wonderland it is any other season of the year. I think that because the weather is so perfect here in Palmville, we have earthquakes to remind us that life is supposed to be faulty (if it were truly perfect, we'd be living in heaven).

OBSERVATION: Mother Earth is a complicated personality. I try to think kindly of her right now and remember the good times, like the long stretches of warm days and breezy, mild nights. But honestly, since the earthquake it's hard for me to be patient with her attitude.

A car pulls up next to us and honks its horn loudly, shaking me out of my deep thoughts. It's the Clamdigger clan. Amy is in the front seat of her mom's spotless and gargantuan car, which is bigger than most people's living rooms. Her older twin brothers and two younger sisters are in the front and middle rows, and her scary oldest brother, Chester, lurks in the back row all by himself, hidden in the shadows.

Through the open window, Amy excitedly reports, "Miss Killjoy is giving out extra credit to any kid who does community service while school is out. I can't believe myself. I've already saved two kittens, delivered fresh water to the Sunshine and Flowers old folks' home, swept the steps at the Palmville Community Center, and now my mom is taking the whole family to volunteer at Palmville Memorial Hospital. I'm one hundred and twenty percent about respect, compassion, and kindness."

Then the light turns green, but Indigo doesn't accelerate. She and Mrs. C are busy sharing earthquake-damage stories with each other. This gives Amy more bragging time.

Amy shouts over to me, "Did you hear about the Make Palmville Beautiful Again Picnic on Sunday? You're supposed to bring your best idea on how to handle earthquakes and the mess they bring with them to the Palmville Council. I can't wait to stun the judges with my originality. If you're chosen, you win a prize. BTW, P, I'm so glad you survived! Wasn't there something groundbreaking in your life you wanted to tell me? Something mysterious, like you were becoming a spy or a detective?"

I quickly respond, "No ground is breaking. Nothing is being detected." I stop myself right there, hoping that Indigo doesn't notice my conspicuous behavior. I look over at her, and thankfully, she's still conversing with Amy's mom.

Indigo finishes her chat with Mrs. C, and finally switches into gear. I gesture out the window for Amy to keep her enthusiasm down to a 1.2. But all I can see now is the Clamdigger car's license plate, which spells P-E-R-F-E-C-T, fade away in the distance.

> **IMPORTANT DATA:** Amy C definitely has a problem with keeping major facts about her best friend's private life secret. She's so public domain about everything!

Chapter 6

Turning the corner to The Tent, we pass our local Internet café, Bits and Bytes. There's a bulky handwritten sign on the door that boasts THE SERVER IS UP! Of course the supernerds have figured out a way to stay wired even without electricity. Webster Holiday, the boy genius in Miss Killjoy's class with the crystalline green eyes, who happens to also be my study partner, is first in line. I wave to him, but he's oblivious. I deduce that the reason Webster doesn't wave back is because he is sneezing uncontrollably, so his vision is most likely blurred. He couldn't possibly be ignoring me, could he?

Suddenly, the hybrid stops short. Silence. Indigo looks into my eyes and announces with fire-engine-red intensity, "Portia, life is going to change for the Avatars."

She knows about my discovery. The missing secret photograph and my mission to find Patch! Now I'll have to confess everything, and I haven't even worked out my confession speech yet. The case is over before it's even begun! I say nothing at all.

Indigo continues, "It's ruined."

That's when I do the math. I look over at what had been until yesterday a cheery health food restaurant with a painted rainbow sign and bougainvillea crawling around the walls like it was doing a snake dance from a distant land. Now what I see is a sorrowful sight. Broken windows, uprooted stairs, and rusty-colored water trickling out of a bent pipe onto the sidewalk. Indigo's livelihood and a piece of her heart now looks like an ad for a disaster relief fund. My heart sinks the way Indigo's must be sinking right now too. I catch myself taking an incredibly deep breath when I think about what's ahead for both of us.

Hap arrives at the scene, carefully opening The Tent's front door, acting uncharacteristically manly as he says in an unfamiliar low voice, "Watch your step, ladies."

As we enter The Tent, I'm relieved to see it's not a total disaster. Even though many of the unmatched wooden tables and individually painted chairs are turned upside down and the walls are cracked in more places than I can count, it's not like the roof caved in or anything. Then Hap and I hear Indigo scream from the back bathroom, "The roof caved in. This is a catastrophe!"

FACT: Indigo has worked really hard every day to make The Tent a destination for the Palmville public to eat healthy food in a serene and fragrant environment. She opened it a few years ago after working at the town's health food store, Naturally Natural. Since then it's been transforming on a daily basis. Many of The Tent's amazingly healthy surprises contain vegetables and herbs she picks from our own garden in the backyard. I'm pretty sure Indigo dreams about this place too, because once in the middle of the night she shouted from her bedroom, "Try mixing the miso with fresh lime!"

Rushing across the dining area, I find her now sitting at her desk in the mouse-size back office surrounded by invoices, old menus, and receipts, all out of order and spread out in every corner of the room.

My hunch earlier this morning was correct: My life will never be the same. Indigo's place of business has been turned inside out. Who's going to lend a hand to my only mother, who is in need of assistance? This is where a father in the house would really come in handy. I can't believe I'm actually feeling angry right now. Not the bloodcurdling sort of anger, but a feeling that can only be described as mad and sad at the same time. I lean over to my nervous-looking mom and embrace her. "What can I do to help?"

IMPORTANT NOTE: I wonder if Patch senses that his family is in trouble right now. People who are really close, like twins, have a feeling when the other one is sick or when something truly groundbreaking is happening to one of them. Even if they're miles away from each other, they know when there's an emotional twister wreaking havoc.

Where are you, Patch? Are you really coming home? If you can hear me, I'd like you to know that if you were ever to choose a time to return to Palmville, this would be it.

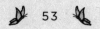

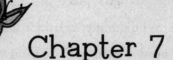

Chapter 7

12:15 P.M.,
CONTENTMENT

Portia's Official List of Contentment
Surviving Food and Beverage Items
(So Far)

17 containers of decaf chai tea

12 gallons of original organic rice milk

3/4 cup of Contentment's own homemade ginger-apple granola (unfortunately, the granola sustained heavy losses)

12 boxes of raw carrots

1 crate of watermelon radishes

As the inventory grows, so does my concern about successfully pursuing my very important case, which is still very much pending.

I glance over at Hap, who stands at the counter preparing lunch for us. He's staring at Indigo while he slices up some of the surviving tomatoes, onions, and peppers. I'm worried for his safety, but I guess sous-chefs are used to chopping while having other more important matters on their minds. Hap's "I'm so in love" glances shoot across the room to Indigo, who sits at one of the newly repaired wooden tables examining large quantities of drinking glasses, checking for chips and cracks, unaware of his intense longing for her. Hap's eyes sparkle when he looks at her. It's almost supernatural.

IMPORTANT QUESTION: Was that the way Patch looked at Indigo over a decade ago when he saw her for the first time?

If my PDA wasn't so low on batteries, I'd consider inputting this new thought into my folder labeled POSSIBLE LIFE-CHANGING TRUTHS. For now I'll make a mental note

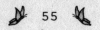

that I should consider sparkling eyes a possible clue about the mystery of my mother and father's first romantic encounter.

Because of this crazy earthquake, it appears that I'll be spending more time in Indigo's universe than usual. So I figure that the more I learn about the many sides of Indigo, the closer I'll get to uncovering the truth about Patch.

MORE QUESTIONS: Why is Indigo so secretive about the story of my conception? Why does she pretend to know so little about Patch, the father of her only child?

Indigo looks up from one of the glasses she is scrutinizing and calls to me. "Portia, are you finished with that last inventory?"

I reply with a secret of my own. "Yes, Mom."

Rubbing her eyes and letting out a deep sigh, she says, "Let's take a break for lunch, and then I'd like you to make some headway in the back office."

I look at her, daydreaming that she instead said, *Perfect, Portia. You've been a huge help. Hap and I can finish up now. You go ahead and spend the day any way you'd like.*

However, life is a lot harsher than most daydreams, and it's pretty obvious that The Tent is going to need all the help it can get. I catch Indigo smiling at me. I think, although no one can ever truly read another person's mind, that this time her smile means that she might be just a little bit proud of me for helping her out in her time of need. She reaches over and hugs me. I hug her back. We sit there together in silence for what seems like a week and a half. The more I try to recall what The Tent looked like before the quake, the foggier the picture gets in my mind.

1:47 P.M.,

CONTENTMENT BACK OFFICE

I sit cross-legged, Indian-style, surrounded by a mountain of paper, ink pens, file folders, stamps, glue sticks, honey-sweetened cough drops, lightbulbs, and rice paper menus. Why did Indigo think I would be even halfway qualified to organize her office? She's seen my room. She knows I have my own unique definition of "cleanliness."

Then a beam of light shines through, hitting the corner of my face. It's as if the sun is trying desperately to make me feel better about the current state of things. I close my eyes, soaking in the warm touch of the fiery ball that sits high up in the sky. My eyes open slowly, like I am awakening from a dream after a long night's sleep. Underneath a severely chipped paper clip holder with an elephant painted on one side, I see a shiny object reflecting back at the sun. I lean over to pick it up and discover it's one of Indigo's stray earrings. I place it in the Japanese bowl at my side that contains other random finds.

I continue creating order out of chaos to the silence of no electricity. I stack invoices for organic sesame sticks, vanilla soy milk, and unbleached rice flour that I find balancing precariously on a monster pile of recycled paper folders. Slowly, the pile loses its balance and topples back down again to the floor. Gravity can be so uncool! I'm 99.99 percent sure that piling up file folders is not my calling.

I make the best of the situation by remaining calm while I collect the folders again. As I do this, I think about the case. I try to picture my father, Patch, when he was my age. Would he have been an art geek, a computer nerd, or a superjock? I bet he was funny, and I know he was extremely popular. I'm sure he was a clean-faced boy who played guitar and baseball. All the girls swarmed around him like bumblebees, wanting just to be in his presence. He was most certainly the teacher's pet. And throughout it all, he wore that hat tipped just over his forehead.

I adjust my magenta cap as images of what Patch might have looked like as a boy pass through my mind. Then I reach for yet another pile of folders. The one that lands at the top of the pile this time is labeled CONFIDENTIAL. The letters are written in bold red ink.

QUESTION: Would Indigo keep personal papers at work?

On cue, my PDA comes to life. It's ringing a funky beat that Amy customized on my phone when I wasn't looking one day at lunch. The Clamdigger has a definite talent for dramatic timing. Is that something a person is born with, or can it be learned in books or on the Internet?

"Portia, I'm calling from the hospital."

I stare at the CONFIDENTIAL label on the folder tab, so I'm only half listening. "What?"

"Hello? Remember, my entire family is volunteering? Anyhow, all the sickies have had their lunch now, but I'm going to keep my fairy wings on to see how many countless others I can save in their time of need."

"Sounds great, Amy." I'm trying to figure out a way to cut this conversation short so I can focus on opening the folder and seeing what secrets are hiding inside.

Amy continues, oblivious to my total lack of enthusiasm about all of her good deeds. "BTW, we passed The Tent on the way to the hospital. I'm sooooo sorry about all the crazy damage. It looks really serious. Are you guys going out of business?"

A sudden chill runs through my body. I quickly respond, "Of course not!" Truthfully, that depressing thought never entered my mind, but now that it's there, it's stuck like bubble gum on the sole of my favorite pair of shoes.

IMPORTANT NOTE: Of course! Indigo's atypical behavior must mean that she's worried about losing her beloved Contentment.

QUESTIONS: What would we do if she ever had to close it down? What would happen to us? Would Indigo have to go back to working behind the counter at Naturally Natural?

I can hear Amy tapping her cell phone. "P, can you hear me? Testing, testing, Portia Avatar, are you even listening?" There's a rustling sound for a few seconds, then Amy returns to the phone again, clearly annoyed and exasperated. "Oh, jeez, one of the sickies is calling out for cranberry juice. Gotta go."

"Okay, Ame."

"Wait! Very important question: Have you become a detective?"

"Uh-huh."

"That's what I thought. Oops. My wings are twitching. A helpless human is in trouble somewhere. Probably the lady in Room 221 who's screeching for the cranberry juice. Ta-ta for now."

Before I can say, *Amy, I'm facing the biggest challenge of my young life, and I think I might have found a major clue about my missing father that could change the course of my personal history,* the red light on my ordinarily trusty PDA disappears, and I'm no longer connected to Amy or to anyone in the outside world for that matter. I'm on my own.

Chapter 8

Breathing deeply, counting my heartbeat: *one, two, three, four . . . seventeen, eighteen, nineteen.* I brace myself for what I am about to experience. One more breath and I'm ready. I slowly open the confidential folder, keeping one eye closed, not sure if both eyes could handle the contents. Here's exactly what I see:

1. *A prehistoric photo of Indigo when she was my age (what's that doing there?)*
2. *Indigo's Social Security card*
3. *The lease for Contentment*

4. *An antique driver's license, picturing a really short-haired Indigo*

5. *A small folded manila envelope with frayed corners*

The folded envelope is highly suspect.

When something is not meant to be seen by others, nine times out of ten, it's in some form of a disguise. Most spies conceal their identities by changing their hair colors, accents, and dates of birth. Sometimes they wear dark glasses and skulk around as if no one can see them. Those are the amateurs! Because it's entirely obvious that someone is spying when he or she overdresses. The best secret agents/spies/detectives keep it simple. They blend in and don't call attention to themselves. Sometimes they adapt by placing a hat on their heads (like Patch) or by wearing an accessory or two (like a scarf or a cool pair of shoes). But that's as far as it goes. Less is so much more in the world of intrigue.

This looks like an ordinary envelope. There is nothing outstanding or super fantastic about it. Its unimportance is only magnified by the fact that there's no label, address, or postage stamp on it either. My hands tremble at the thought that it contains a clue that might lead to the discovery I've been waiting for since birth.

This moment is radically tense. It's interrupted by muffled music coming from deep within my knapsack. I guess my flaky PDA has decided to work again. Usually, I am thrilled to receive a call, but now it's only a distraction delaying me from having a potentially memorable experience that I might be reminiscing about for years to come.

Of course it's the Clamdigger on the other end. Right on cue. In a rushed voice she begins, "Very important question, P. Have you decided on your idea for the picnic this Sunday? Because I've had about twenty-seven in the last hour."

"Amy, I'm on a case and can't afford any distractions right now." I'm holding the manila envelope tightly in my trembling left hand.

"*Pardonez moi.* It slipped my mind that you're Miss Girl Detective now. But I just can't decide 'cause my ideas are all so extraordinarily original. I thought you might be able to help me."

"This is not the right time."

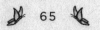

"Don't tell me you're going to let your career get in the way of your personal life."

"My career is my personal life!"

"Whatever. I'll just handle this avalanche of originality all by my lonesome."

"Sorry, Amy, I need to get back to my case."

"I comprehend. That's what friends do. They comprehend."

"Thanks for comprehending. Gotta go."

FACT: I know Amy cares about me, but sometimes she's just a little too "Amy" for me.

I carefully place my hand in the envelope, but there's nothing inside. I'm relieved, which surprises me. But I don't stop there. Just in case I missed anything, I turn the envelope upside down and shake it like an old pair of shoes after a hike in the nearby canyons. A small metal object flies out, landing somewhere between the overturned box of newly printed menus and the spilled garbage bin of duplicate receipts and junk mail. Sifting through the jungle of disorganized office accessories, I spot the metal object. It's a ring, a golden band, and it looks just like a wedding ring, only it's got a funny pattern carved on it.

> **NOTE:** Although my PDA has less than even minimal battery time left, I input a short description of the golden band and its unfamiliar carvings, sensing that this discovery is crucial to the case.

I take the ring and slowly slip it onto the ring finger of my left hand. As I stare out the small window above the cluttered desk, I imagine Indigo the way she looked in the driver's license photograph (young and with short hair) and Patch (who is still blurry to me) holding hands. They are walking down the street, close together, the way I've seen couples do outside Palmville High School. The golden band is now on her ring finger. It shines brightly, reflecting a stream of light from the sun. I catch a fragment of the light reflecting off the rare metal and look down at my hand. The ring almost fits my finger. When I look at my hand again, I see myself growing up.

QUESTIONS: Could this be a clue? Is this Indigo's wedding band? If it is, can I assume that my parents loved each other?

That last question sends shivers all over.

Putting emotions aside and staying focused on the case, I deduce that the answer will be in Indigo's eyes. If they sparkle (the way Hap's do when he looks at her), then I'll know for sure.

PLAN OF ACTION: Find a way to test Indigo on the subject of true love for my missing father, Patch.

I know the truth in my heart, but I need proof. I place the ring back inside the envelope, which I fold over several times until it fits snuggly inside my back pocket. Then I close my eyes and cross my fingers (and toes), praying that my pursuit will lead to the indisputable fact that I am indeed a love child.

Chapter 9

6:19 P.M.,

MY BEDROOM

"Come on, Frederick. It's time to come out now!" My coaxing doesn't lead anywhere, so I try another strategy. "Frederick, since the earthquake I've noticed that nothing in life is ever certain. You might as well get used to that fact."

A loud meow that sounds almost like a bark travels to me from a far corner under my bed. Clearly, he's reaching out to me. Once again I find myself crawling on all fours, covered in dust bunnies, trying to get as close to my nervous Nelly cat as possible. I try to soothe him by sharing the newest development in the case. He stops meowing when I mention my discovery of the ring, undoubtedly sensing its significance for the case. Seriously lacking in rest and relaxation, I try hard to keep my eyes open as I recount my day to my kooky little furball, but soon my eyelids shut tight and I'm in complete darkness. All I hear is Frederick's loud purring. A kitty cat lullaby sends me deep into sleep.

6:35 P.M.,

MY BEDROOM, A DREAM

I am in a faraway place. Wind sweeps across a great desert. The sounds are foreign to me. I hear a camel cry in the distance. I try to shout to calm him, but my voice is buried by the swirling wind and sand. Then I turn and see a person standing on top of a nearby dune. It's me. I wave to myself. I look down at my left hand and see that I am holding something. It's a postcard. On the front of the card is a picture of an Indian dancer with bracelets on her ankles and wrists. The other side is truly mysterious. I know it's from Patch. I think I can make out what it says.

Portia, my lovely daughter.
Home seems far away, but always
in my heart. Look for me with every rising sun.
Your loving father

Even though I have no idea where I am or where my next glass of water will come from, I feel totally at home. *DREAM ENDS*.

6:49 P.M.,

MY BEDROOM

Wind chimes stir me out of my sleep. That signals dinnertime. I find Frederick kneading my stomach, testing that his claws still work. They do! I don't mind because the fact that he's not hiding anymore is a major breakthrough.

I carefully slide out from under the bed, holding Frederick in my arms. I've got big plans to celebrate his bravery for leaving his treasured hiding place. Festivities include leftover catnip from his last birthday party (Frederick is a Pisces, BTW).

Suddenly, the floor beneath my feet starts to tremble. Then it stops. Indigo from downstairs: "Just another aftershock. Everything okay up there?"

"Fine, Mom."

Without missing a beat, she adds, "Dinner is ready!"

"Be right down."

Frederick squirms out from my hands and returns to his own prison of fear. It's not just another aftershock to him. It's more like the world is overwhelming him and he's completely lost all control of his former life.

I check my PDA, which seems to be working, although the batteries are fading fast. I quickly input my notes about Frederick's extreme behavior for a future case.

IDENTIFYING DATA

SUBJECT: Freddy Fred Frederick Avatar. Approximately six years old (was found at the animal shelter as a kitten at approximately eight weeks old). 12.5 pounds. Long body, gray-and-white patterned fur. Short legs, long tail, and extra-long whiskers. One distinguishing yellow front tooth and one ripped left ear caused by a fight with a neighbor's cat over a boundary issue.

NATURE OF CONTACT: Guardian, nurturer, and "owner" of subject.

LENGTH OF CONTACT: Since subject was a kitten.

THE PROBLEM: Subject exhibits the following symptoms: extreme fear of earthquakes.

BACKGROUND MATERIAL: Subject abandoned by both birth parents. Loves to sleep on couch arms, feather pillows, and television sets.

DIAGNOSTIC CATEGORY: Small Pet Nervous Disorder.

METHODS: More investigation and patience.

From downstairs, Indigo calls for me again. "Portia?"

"Coming!"

*I*ndigo has attempted to make dinner without any electricity or gas. She appears to have succeeded. Grabbing the flashlight, she signals for me to try one of her raw food appetizers. By candlelight I sample a fresh mint and kelp stuffed tomato (yum!). She then takes the flashlight and heads outside to cut a few sprigs of cilantro from the herb garden for the main course: flaxseed hero sandwiches (double yum!).

I make a silent promise to myself that as soon as Indigo walks back into the kitchen, I will try to find a way to mention Patch's name in conversation. When I do, my eyes will be fixed on hers. If I see a "love sparkle" shoot out like a private fireworks show, then I'll know for sure that Indigo was in love with Patch.

NOTE: This totally enlightening day has put me through more major tests than I would have taken in three months at Palmville Middle School.

Tests So Far

1. *Keeping a major secret from Indigo about finding the hidden photo of Patch*

2. *Trying to stay focused on my super-emotional Man of Many Hats case*

3. *Remaining patient with a cat who not only thinks he's a dog, but who's got a seemingly incurable nervous condition*

4. *Tolerating my talkative friend, Amy Clamdigger*

5. *Discovering, then "borrowing," what appears to be Indigo's wedding ring!*

6. *Maintaining a calm, cool, and collected demeanor when at any point I might learn* The Absolute Complete Unabridged Version of the History of Indigo and Patch

From outside, I hear Indigo shout to me. "Portia, please set the table, sweetheart. Dinner is about to be served."

"Most certainly."

Indigo enters from the back, holding two handfuls of freshly picked, fragrant cilantro. "What was that you said?"

Why did I say "most certainly"? How random. I've never used those two words together in a sentence in my life. I shake myself out of dweebette mode and repeat several times to myself, *I must appear normal, I must appear normal, I must appear normal,* even if I don't feel that way. So I respond to her by simply saying, "Yes, Mom."

"Thanks, honey. That would be a big help."

I set the table while Indigo puts the finishing touches on her signature mango gazpacho. The exotic nutrient-filled soup will precede the flaxseed sandwiches (joy!).

Indigo's Post-Earthquake Dinner Menu

Fresh Organic Mint and Sea Kelp
Stuffed Tomatoes

Cool Mango Gazpacho

Flaxseed Hero Sandwiches
with Backyard Cilantro

Three-Day-Old Cranberry
Oatmeal Cookies

FACT: I plan to fill up on the mango soup because the thought of flaxseed ANYTHING at such a critical juncture in my life (and career) is NOT very appetizing.

As Indigo serves the colorful cold soup, I watch her every move—the way she tilts the spoon, her grip on the handle, her mindful eyes. She catches me staring at her.

I start the dinner conversation tonight. "I was trying to calm Frederick down a little while ago and dozed off under my bed."

"That's wonderful. You caught up on some dream time. Anything to report?"

I offer the Dream Checker this: "Yes! I had the most super-amazing dream ever!"

Furrowing her brow and looking at me straight in the eyes, she says, "Really?"

IMPORTANT NOTE: This is the perfect opportunity to test Indigo's love for Patch.

I continue, "I was in the high desert, far away from everything that was familiar. Only the craziest thing was that I saw myself standing on a nearby dune. So I started waving to myself. That's when I noticed it in my hand."

"Noticed what?"

"The postcard from him."

Playing it incredibly clueless, she asks, "Who?"

"Patch! It was another postcard from Patch. The dream means that Patch is coming home this time, Mom. I know it!"

Each time I mention Patch's name, I look for the sparkle in Indigo's eyes, but because of the candlelight and the serious lack of electricity, it's hard to see clearly.

Indigo puts on her stern-mother face. "Now, Portia, dreams can be interpreted in a number of ways. There's a rainbow of possible meanings there."

"Well, this one was so sparkly crystal clear, I know it's true."

"I'm sure the postcard was a symbol of something going on in your life."

"Why don't you let me interpret my own dream?" Defiantly, I continue, "Patch is on his way home!"

That's when I see it. The sparkle in Indigo's eyes, reflecting the emotional truth buried deep inside her soul.

Right now she's probably imagining my dad and her husband, Patch, and pondering the love that links the three of us together. The sparkle morphs into a reflection from an unknown visitor's flashlight coming through our kitchen window.

Who is this evening intruder?

Chapter 10

7:32 P.M.,

AVATAR KITCHEN

The flashlight intruder's name is Rock Neruda. His job is to put out fires, clean his truck, and save little kitties from tree branches. In other words, he's a fire-fighter. Evidently, he's touring the neighborhood, checking on all the houses to see if we need any free-of-charge tips about fire safety after the earthquake. Supposedly, he's here to check on gas leaks or exposed electrical wiring and to answer any questions we might have about preparedness and response.

Indigo giggles as she eyes his overly developed arm muscles, then says, "I have a question."

Rock responds with a great burst of energy. "Shoot!"

"Will you join me and my daughter, Portia, for dinner? It's not much, but—"

Before she can even finish her sentence, he jumps in. "I'd love nothing more. Thank you, Mrs. Avatar."

Lowering her eyes and the volume of her voice: "Just call me Indigo."

"Indigo, I must say I have never seen such a spread within twenty-four hours of a major earthquake." Then he looks over to me. "Portia, your mom is really something."

I reply with a little bit of pepper and a lot of cayenne, "I think so."

All through dinner I watch Indigo transform herself into someone I do not recognize as my mother. Normally, she's extremely mellow, quietly asking me questions about my day. But tonight she's hyped up, speaking louder than usual and shifting in her seat a lot. Also, there is nothing particularly funny about Rock, so I keep wondering why she laughs at his express train of bad jokes.

From his first taste of cold mango soup, Rock instantly

makes himself at home. Leaning back in "his" chair with his long legs stretched out, he starts sharing stories about the neighbors and local businesses that have been affected by the quake. "In my experience, it's difficult times like these that bring communities together."

Indigo nods in an exaggerated way to make sure that Rock will pick up on the fact that she absolutely agrees with every word he says. "Yes, I notice that too."

Rock seems to like the sound of his own voice, and neither Indigo nor I am stopping him, so he just keeps on talking. "This is the time when families who have been apart for long periods of time reach out to one another and reunite."

QUESTIONS: Could this be a new clue? How could Rock possibly know that I am in the process of putting together the reunion of a lifetime?

NOTE: Perhaps this firefighter guy, who sits a little too close to my mother, knows slightly more about the workings of the world than just how to steer a fire truck. Still, I'll need more convincing.

 82

*D*essert is served. A plate of cranberry oatmeal cookies Indigo baked three days ago, but they still taste pretty good (they are not Oreos, however). Mr. Earthquake Hero wolfs down two at once.

QUESTION: Doesn't Rock ever stop eating?

It occurs to me that maybe he's been busy today, saving people and calming nerves after the earthquake. That probably explains his extreme state of hunger. I watch as his energy level just keeps accelerating with each story he tells us. Indigo is all ears (and eyes).

Somewhere during the marathon conversation Rock mentions that Vera Alloway, owner of Trash and Treasures, the local junk shop, got hit hard and could use some outside help.

Indigo chimes in, "Portia, isn't there something Amy said this morning about extra credit for doing good deeds

83

in the community? I think helping Vera would be a great idea."

NOTE: I thought Indigo wasn't listening to my conversation with Amy in the car this morning. Could that mean that she overheard Amy's comment about me being a detective?

Rock adds his three cents. "Indigo is right. That's just what Palmville needs right now. Positive community action!"

QUESTIONS: Has anybody seen my barf bag? Since when does Rock have any authority over my free days? Who does he think he is—my father?

I make believe that I am sincerely interested in spending my valuable time in a junk shop with a dust problem that promises to be twenty times as severe as the one at home. Conjuring up a few sneezes for effect, I agree to help out. "Sure, Mom."

Rock leans even farther back in his chair, his hands folded behind his head, like he owns the place and is satisfied with my response (as if he played some leading role in my decision to get extra credit).

This firefighter guy is officially bugging me. Aren't there any fires waiting to be put out? Maybe nearby homeowners and apartment renters need a lecture on how to turn off their gas valves and stay away from loose hanging objects? Why does Rock pick this evening, this house, and my mom to flaunt his "charming" ways? I am not fooled for a millisecond.

I excuse myself from the table with a credible cover story. "Indigo, I need to bring Frederick his dinner. I'm supremely positive that he is most likely starving right about now."

Rock smiles. "That sounds serious."

Without missing a beat, I say, "It is. He's got small pet nervous disorder."

Indigo hands me my flashlight without even an eighth of an argument. I am so worthy of an Academy Award when I muster, "Thank you, Rock, for visiting our modest dwelling and for making us wise to the ways of post-earthquake hazards." Then I gracefully (at least I think so) make my Hollywood exit.

Indigo looks at me with a combination of shock, confusion, and pride. Then her face softens. She's clearly fallen for my adorable daughter performance. Her smile broadens with each passing second. "Good night, sweet Portia."

Chapter 11

8:31 P.M.,

MY BEDROOM

My ancient flashlight guides me up the stairs to my bedroom. It's clear as soon as I walk inside the dark room, lit only by the distant moon outside my window, that Frederick's digestive system is unmistakably working. I detect a highly suspicious smell coming from the direction of the bathroom. That must mean he actually left his secret hiding place at some point during the evening and went to the little boys' room. And guess who's on cleanup committee? Lucky me!

With three store-bought treats I found hidden in one of the kitchen drawers clenched securely in my right fist, I crawl into the darkness to join him under my bed. That's when my PDA decides to work again. There appears to be a message waiting for me.

My PDA's constant malfunctioning reminds me that we are still in earthquake recovery mode. The on-again, off-again telephone and wireless connections only call attention to the chaos that's just outside. Helicopters hover overhead. No night owl or even a stray cricket, just the random and occasional shouting of neighbors fills the eerie silence of an electricity-less Palmville.

Two fire engines pass our house. I wonder if Rock isn't just 85 percent concerned that he's missing out on yet another heroic deed, or is he still bragging to Indigo about more of his superhuman feats?

I feed Frederick the treats that I scavenged from the

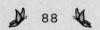

kitchen. He crunches loudly in delight. His purring increases in volume with each bite. Everything under the bed at the moment seems to be excellent — considering. As I squirm back out into the open air of my ridiculously untidy room, I check the message on my PDA. It's from Amy (big surprise!).

Although my batteries are now tragically low and the electricity is in the same state of nothingness that it was this morning, I yearn to make a connection. Even if it's just words and symbols on an impossibly small screen, I must reach out now or I'll implode.

Amy's message is shorter than I was anticipating:

My hair despises earthquakes. :-(Text me!
Ame

Throwing all concerns of reserve battery time out the window, I start texting furiously. I had no idea that being a detective and keeping my mouth shut for so long would make me so lonely!

My message to Amy has significantly more words than hers:

 89

U will not in a centennial believe my day. My first and most important case, about my missing father, Patch, has led me down various dead ends and blind alleys. But I found a ring, OMG! Yes, I think it's theirs (translation: Indigo's and Patch's wedding ring). I saw a sparkle in Indigo's eyes when I mentioned Patch's name, so I'm pretty sure that means they really truly loved each other. Then this mysterious new (unwanted) stranger who calls himself Rock appeared from nowhere. :C He's a firefighter the Santa Ana winds blew in about an hour ago. BTW, he actually came in through the back door. :-O. Remember that the above information is highly confidential. I hope you have a shake-free sleep. P

Amy replies:

Your new career sounds cool! You're so totally Jamie Bondette. No worries, I adore secrets. I will keep my lips sealed. Promise!

GNSD.

Suddenly, my temporary happy mood is interrupted by a slight rumbling under my feet. That's not fair! Another earthquake so soon would be too much to handle in one twenty-four-hour period! I let out a big sigh and lean back, letting myself fall onto my bed. My back lands on the brightly printed pink and purple bedspread Indigo bought me last year for my eleventh birthday. As my legs leave the floor, I pretend I am floating in space weightless, without a worry in the world. For a moment I let today leave my body just to see what it feels like to let go.

I calm myself when I realize that what I was feeling wasn't an earthquake at all. It wasn't even an aftershock. It was just a gray-and-white kitty cat named Frederick discovering a new hiding-in-terrible-fear position under my bed while he prepares for sleep. I whisper softly, "I'm tired too. Good night, Frederick."

I change out of my dirty earthquake cleanup clothes

and get ready for bed. Dodging the random objects that sit on my rug, I yearn to find suitable sleepwear. Outside my window, which is still covered in plaster and dust, I hear garbled voices and then a high-pitched giggle. Rock must be leaving — finally!

I peer out from the bottom corner of the window, careful not to make myself easily visible. Then I observe Rock leave the house. I take note of his overly confident gait and the way he smoothly looks over his right shoulder for a second glance at Indigo (like he's forgotten what she looks like or something). If a firefighter could skip down our rocky path, that's what he would do. But because he's a hero type, he strides with a firefighter bop toward his red pickup truck. His headlights go on, and for the first time since sundown, I can see more than four feet ahead of me. Then the sound of a V-8 engine disappears along with the light. It's dark again, the smell of smoke is still in the air, and I'm ready for bed.

Through the open door, I shout to Indigo, "Good night!"

"Happy dreaming!"

"You too." I lean over my bed and calmly tell

Frederick, "Cheer up. This is not as good as it gets."

Then I look out the window at a moon that is just about full.

> **NOTE:** Even after earthquakes, the moon is still as calm and cool as ever.

> **QUESTION:** If Patch were halfway around the world, would the moon be almost full like the one I'm staring at right now, or would it be the opposite—a new moon that is just about to reveal itself?

Chapter 12

My front porch is entirely crooked. The earthquake hasn't helped matters either. As I sit on the top step, which seriously needs a new coat of paint, I stare at the mailbox at the end of the stone path and think back to all the dreams I've had of postcards sent to me from my father. These postcards are always treasures buried beneath piles of glossy catalogues, junk mail, bills, and the occasional invitation. Each is scented with the aroma of spices from faraway places. There is always a short message of love from him on one side. And on the other, an exotic and beautiful image.

The photograph, the sparkle in Indigo's eyes, and the carved golden ring are all signs that Patch has roamed the earth but is still (for some reason) in traveling mode. I feel so close to finding my missing father right now, I can hardly stand it. Looking left, right, and over my shoulder, too, I slip my hand inside my back pocket and take out my newest piece of evidence—the ring. I study it in the morning light. My focus zooms in on the unfamiliar carvings. I'm sure they must have some special meaning. Maybe these curious markings are part of still another clue to explore.

I take out my PDA and input my thoughts as fast as my fingers can type. I'm surprised to discover more battery life left. The digital display reads 9:30 a.m. That's when Indigo wanted to go over to The Tent this morning.

Then I'm not sure what takes over me, but some force bigger and stronger than I am lifts me up and sends me rushing to check the mailbox, just in case I missed something yesterday.

There's nothing.

At first I'm disappointed, but then I remember that there's been an earthquake, and the mail service isn't up to speed quite yet. Patch's next postcard detailing his return is coming. It's just stuck in a pile temporarily backed up because of all the shaking that's been going on.

9:35 A.M.,

PALMVILLE STREET

I guess Palmville is a pretty okay place to live, except for the earthquakes, when the ground does that strange dance. Today, as Indigo and I make the drive to The Tent, the sun beats down over the red Spanish rooftops that creep and crawl along the hills. In many ways it seems like an ordinary day.

I look out the window, observing more of the effects from the earthquake. The traffic lights are still not working. People in their cars try to be as polite as they can be under the circumstances, but the tension seeps through their closed doors and windows in pretty obvious ways. Right now there's a woman behind us who keeps beeping her horn. Does she really expect us to cause an accident because she's in a hurry? Where is she going, anyway? I deduce that she's just hit with a strong case of post-earthquake nerves, so I forgive her rude behind-the-wheel behavior.

On the way I notice that there's a larger group huddled outside Bits and Bytes than yesterday. And there's Webster again. For a computer geek, he's kind of cute. Our four-door cruises slowly past the café. I discreetly take out the carved ring from my pocket. Clutching it in the palm of my left hand, I gather up the courage to shout to him through the open window, "Where are you going, Webster?"

QUESTION: Why in the entire universe did I just ask that?

It's strange, but I notice that since the earthquake my boldness factor has increased by at least 29 percent.

Of course Webster is going to Bits and Bytes. He's standing directly in front of the open door! What am I thinking? Mortification central.

To my complete surprise, he responds, "I'm heading to the lithosphere! On my way to predicting earthquakes and saving the world from . . . natural disasters."

Clueless as to what and where the lithosphere is and how an eleven-year-old kid (Webster skipped a grade) could ever possibly predict an earthquake, I shout back to him, "Have a great trip!"

Convinced that I have just made a total fool of myself, I melt into my seat, trying futilely to cover myself in my seat belt. As if that's really going to work. I slowly sink below the window and get an insight on my way down to my not-so-clever hiding place. The Internet! With the Needle in a Haystack search engine, I can find anything—even a missing father.

I bolt up straight in plain view once again, my thoughts flying in every direction. I try to catch them one at a time. As I do this, I glance over at Indigo, who is thankfully unaware of my scheming. She's looking straight ahead with a smile on her face, lost in her own thoughts, although I'm 98 percent sure her thoughts are not half as earth-shattering as mine are at this very moment. This morning's smile is hard to interpret. But I do wonder if Indigo's more lighthearted mood has anything to do with last night's intruder.

My Next Plan of Action

A) *Sneak away from The Tent*

B) *Travel the World Wide Web to determine Patch's whereabouts*

I feel the warmth of the sun, which is shining brightly. I can almost hear it tell me, *You're right on track, Portia! Don't give up.* Today promises to overflow with milestones. I pray the batteries on my PDA hold out.

Chapter 13

A tall, buff figure like a cowboy (only no hat) leans confidently on the sign that reads:

CONTENTMENT

VEGETARIAN CUISINE FOR THE
MIND, BODY, AND SOUL.

Parked right in front of The Tent is a bright red truck. Can you guess the identity of this mysterious figure?

QUESTION: Why is it that firefighters are so obsessed with the color red?

Indigo's face softens when she sees Rock. My face turns a bright shade of pink. I am embarrassed for my mother, who is spinning around like a top in front of this so-called hero. How completely ridiculous! Rock has supposedly come by this morning to teach Indigo how to turn off the gas and prevent post-earthquake fires in the restaurant (I thought he taught her that last night?). His eyes sparkle when he looks at her. I pretend not to notice that fact.

But Hap does. He pulls up in his VW that only a mother could love, the engine choking and stuttering to a halt. He sits frozen in the driver's seat staring at Indigo and Rock's flirtatious tango. Even through the windshield, I can see his face turn an ashen gray, the same color of the dust that's been seeping through our walls at home and The Tent since the earthquake. Beads of sweat form around his forehead. One drops on the tip of his nose, waking him from his very own living nightmare.

Meanwhile, Indigo giggles as she unsuccessfully attempts to open the front door with her key. "Oh dear, this key doesn't seem to be working."

Hap observes this and attempts to leap from his Bug,

but he gets caught in his seat belt. He quickly untangles himself and rushes "to the rescue." Rock looks on with a sly smile plastered on his face. He turns to Indigo. "Do you even know this guy?"

Indigo smiles. "That's Hap, my sous-chef."

Ignoring Rock completely, Hap tries desperately to look like the man-in-charge as he turns the key with all his strength. When he finally unlocks the door, he stumbles forward, falling into a pile of dust. He lets out a loud sneeze that sends Indigo into a deeper state of giggles. Rock joins in with his own brand of uncontrollable laughter.

FACT: Hap does not find the situation funny in the least.

This time after Indigo walks around her home away from home, she isn't distracted by the heap of broken furniture, cracked walls, and spilled bags of brown rice and black beans that still cover the dining area's floor. She's preoccupied with a friendly firefighter. Hap notices this too and immediately switches gears, from sweet, gentle poetic type to squinty-eyed jealous type. Then he sneezes again and disappears into the back bathroom to wash up.

As this unexpected love triangle starts to form its opposing angles, I seize the opportunity to slip out through the beaded entrance. My ultra cool move does not go unnoticed by Indigo. She peaks through the hanging beads and says sweetly, "You're going to Trash and Treasures, right? Vera could really use your help."

Forcing an angelic smile: "Sure, Mom. That's exactly where I'm going. See you later."

As I leave The Tent, I glance back through the window and notice that Hap is now cleaned up and sweeping the floor in a repetitive manner. He's staring at Rock while simultaneously missing large piles of uncooked rice and dried beans. I think that maybe this firefighter guy has turned Hap's life upside down—just a little.

Chapter 14

I use all the Palmville insider's shortcuts, sailing through town, past the Cappuccino Café, which usually turns out aromatic mochas all through the day (and night). However, slightly more than twenty-four hours after the earthquake there's no smell of steaming double cappuccinos or iced caramel decaf creams. Life is still not even a centimeter closer to being normal.

I've walked past Trash and Treasures for about a hundred years, but I've never actually stepped inside. Vera Alloway, Palmville's junk connoisseur, is the owner and operator of this extremely dusty establishment. When she's not selling her beloved "trash and treasures," she's making art out of them. The front entrance of her shop is an ever-evolving junkyard paradise, featuring Coke can trees with pipe branches and bottle cap leaves. She has created outdoor furniture made from olive oil tins and soda bottles and has padded the chairs with old movie theater seat cushions. She has even planted a vegetable garden of metal scraps that she regularly waters with spoons and buttons.

10:25 A.M.,

TRASH AND TREASURES

A hand-painted sign hangs on an antique hat rack just inside the front door:

EVERY DISCARDED OBJECT DESERVES A HOME
CASH ONLY!

As soon as I enter the shop, Vera calls out from behind a rack of worn leather jackets. "Is that the young and highly inquisitive Portia Avatar?"

How can she see me from behind those coats?

Vera then appears in plain sight, clutching an old bird-cage she's trying to salvage. "Your mother told me you'd be coming."

> **QUESTION:** How did Indigo manage to call Vera when our phones are dead at home and her cell phone is down too? This curious fact needs further investigation.

Switching back to my conversation with Vera, I try out my "I'm so enthusiastic" routine. "What can I do to help?"

"Well, cookie, just look around and start anywhere."

Checking my lemon yellow plastic daisy wristwatch and trying hard to figure out how and when I can slip away to search the Internet for my long-lost father, I keep up my "I'm so happy to be here" smile. "Absolutely, Vera."

Vera appears to totally buy my act, because now she's all smiles too.

 106

DESCRIPTION: Vera Alloway is about sixty years old. She's a desert queen with a tanned, wrinkly face. She's tall, long-legged, and wears a bandanna on her head. She always wears lots of silver jewelry she makes herself. Each creation is hand-crafted from select pieces of junk from her shop. And it is rumored that Vera is the most psychic person in Palmville!

I look around Palmville's junk museum. My educated guess is that Trash and Treasures has always been disorganized, but now it's way high on the Richter scale of messiness. I pass stained lampshades, diamond-studded platform shoes, flowery housedresses, leisure suits, torn couches, and bicycle wheels until I finally spot my first patient—a broken vase.

Bending down to the dusty floor to collect the pieces of the clay vase, I carefully throw each one into a nearby garbage bin. I'm feeling totally productive, fulfilling my community service duty while at the same time making sense of this overwhelming topsy-turvydom.

Vera snakes her hands through a maze of rusted toasters, silver lipstick holders, and souvenir ashtrays to slowly and meticulously reach down and take out the pieces of the vase from the garbage bin, placing them on a nearby counter—one by one.

She hands me a plastic bottle of glue and calmly explains, "Sometimes things are more beautiful with age, cracks, and scars. It's hard putting the pieces back together again, but it's worth it. Did you know that every object has its own special story? In the future please don't throw out anything without checking with me first. Got it?"

I was just trying to do Vera a favor and it backfired. Community service certainly has its challenges! Now I'm walking on thin ice, but really it's broken glass, soiled tablecloths, and faded postcards. Whistling has always seemed to calm me down in the past, so I give it a try while attempting to create order out of a disordered pile of rhinestone necklaces.

A couple of hours have passed by the time Vera calls out from the back room, "I hear there are a bunch of kids around your age at Bits and Bytes. Go ahead. You've been of real service today."

I can't believe Vera seems to know exactly where I

wanted to go. I don't give away that I'm just a little freaked out that she can read my mind. "Are you sure?"

QUESTIONS: What's Vera's secret? How can she know so much with so little information? Is she really psychic like everyone says?

I'm at the door within a nanosecond. I shout out a good-bye to Vera, who's still at her desk in the back office.

"I think you forgot this," she shouts.

"What?"

Vera emerges from the darkness. She carefully shuts the door to her office behind her. Before she does, I think I catch a glimpse of some sort of monstrous object back there, but maybe it's my eyes playing tricks on me. What does she do in that office all day, anyway, and what was that thing?

Vera hands me the most stylin', retro cool ocean blue cabbie hat you can imagine. I do a quick head check. Sure enough, I forgot to put on my favorite magenta knitted cap this morning.

I take the new hat and immediately test it out. It fits perfectly. She smiles, then sends me on my way. "I'd love to see you tomorrow, if you can spare the time."

I adjust the hat and then turn to her. "I'm there, V." I reach into my pocket, trying to find something to give Vera in return. All I find is an old nickel I picked up on my way home from pottery class last week. "Here! If a penny is good luck, then I bet a nickel is five times as good!"

"Thank you, Portia. I think we've got a mighty fine trade here! Now off you go!"

I start the short walk down the street to Bits and Bytes, making sure my hat is tipped at just the right angle before I greet the public.

QUESTIONS: Vera says that every discarded object has a story. What's the exciting tale of this hat? If I wear it long enough, will I figure it out?

Then I picture the type of hat Patch is wearing right now. It's a scarf! He's wearing a brightly colored scarf wrapped around his head, protecting himself from the

harsh ultraviolet rays of the burning sun. I close my eyes to help myself visualize him better.

He's on a journey, just like I am, and he's heading home!

As I approach Bits and Bytes, I wonder why I hadn't thought of searching for Patch on the Internet before.

QUESTION: Why did it take a natural disaster to turn me around?

Chapter 15

*A*t Bits and Bytes (aka B&B), Webster and Keithy are involved in a furious video game battle. Webster has evidently taken a break from visiting the lithosphere and solving science's most perplexing mysteries. Now he's focused on outmaneuvering his opponent and scoring massive points. He's wearing a T-shirt that reads GOT DIGITAL? Who dresses him? Maybe because the electricity is out, he couldn't see what he was putting on this morning. I find his goofy T-shirt pretty humorous and decide not to call the fashion police on him—this time.

As the battle rages on, Amy sits loyally next to "her man" Keithy, cheering him on, even though it's clear that he's losing big to Webster, whose knack for video gaming is legendary at Palmville Middle School. Amy claims that Keithy is her "boyfriend" and that they've been together for six whole weeks. But I know for a fact that they haven't even held hands yet. A few days before the earthquake she confided in me that he's her "practice boyfriend" for high school, because that's when she says boyfriends will be seriously valuable commodities.

I wave to Amy, who gives me only half a wave and a mouthed *hi* in return. It seems she's more concerned with acting the part of Keithy's "stand by your man" girlfriend than talking to me, her oldest and best friend.

I look around the café, observing the crowd that has gathered to connect with one another and over the Internet. The unfamiliar buzz of electricity warms the air and my heart. It means that soon I will take my turn at the keyboard to search for clues about Patch.

FACT: The owners of Bits and Bytes lack basic social skills and manners. However, they are forgiven on a daily basis

because their jobs are so important to the Palmville netizens. The only time the B&B guys seem to enjoy conversation is when the subject matter is focused on the innards of a microprocessor. Although they are not brothers, they may as well be since they're identical in almost every way except for hair type (one has curly and the other has straight). Their names are Joe and Ben, and both are twentysomething. They use their genius skills every day to keep Palmville wired and connected to the web.

I spot my media lab teacher, Mr. Scuzzy, who is sitting at a corner table with his laptop, which works only because the B&B geniuses have jury-rigged a stack of wires together. Seeing a teacher outside of school is weird, but nothing in the past few days has been exactly normal. After a long, silent discussion with myself, I decide to say hello to Mr. Scuzzy.

DESCRIPTION: Mr. Scuzzy has long, dark hair. His voice is as smooth as a T3 line. He's way tall, and I don't think he's married (he's missing a gold band on his left ring finger). Also, he's on the young side for a teacher. Today, like almost every

other day, he wears a black T-shirt and a pair of comfortable-looking blue jeans.

I shuffle shyly over to his table. "Hi, Mr. Scuzzy. Glad to see that you survived the earthquake."

He suppresses a smile. "Hi, Portia. Good to see you're okay too."

"I'm here to go on a search."

"What are you looking for?"

ALERT!: What have I done? My secret mission is not for public consumption!

I continue cautiously. "Just searching, you know, for stuff."

"That's cool. Promise me that you'll have a great wired adventure."

Hoping that I haven't revealed the true motive of my Internet search, I mutter, "I promise."

The Clamdigger spies me chatting with Mr. S, which inspires her to break away from her "boyfriend" and approach us. She launches right in. "I'm so

 115

exhausted. This community service thing makes you really, really tired."

Taking the bait, Mr. Scuzzy responds, "What have you been up to, Amy?"

That's my cue to sneak away. I excuse myself politely to wait in line for my turn at one of the nearby computer stations. As I take my place third in line, I think about how I'll begin my search. There are so many directions I can take, but no road map. Total uncharted territory.

My thoughts are interrupted by Amy's high-volume bragging coming from the direction of Mr. Scuzzy's table. Poor Mr. S! He's packing up his computer now, trying to find his way to the nearest exit. Oblivious to the not-so-subtle hint, Amy follows him, going on and on about all the extra credit she's practically guaranteed to get from Miss Killjoy.

Now that Mr. S is gone, Amy looks back over to Keithy. Their eyes meet. He nods and she smiles. But I know there's no love between them because I don't see even a *flicker* of a sparkle.

Meanwhile, Webster notices me from across the room. He shyly nods at me. I find the inner strength to shout from the line, "How's the lithosphere?"

I wonder why I'm behaving so strangely. I'm starting to think that I'm the geek now, not Webster.

Webster responds immediately, without skipping even a sixteenth of a beat. "Crusty."

What does he possibly mean by that? I fake a knowing smile, offering, "That's excellent!"

NOTE: Webster is pretty decent for a boy. Sometimes he reminds me of one of the B&B guys because he clearly spends more time with his LCD screen than he does with people. But maybe that's something a kid can outgrow.

Chapter 16

*E*ons have passed since I first attempted my escape through The Tent's beaded entrance. Sometimes I think mothers are rigged with eyes in the back of their heads and an extra set of ears. I wonder if Indigo is tracking my time away from the restaurant. At some point she will catch on that my community service took a left turn. But I'm convinced that Vera will vouch for me, so for the moment my mission is safe.

Finally, a little bell rings and my number is called. As luck (or fate) would have it, I am assigned the computer station where Webster was working. Since the video game battle ended, Webster has been feverishly research-ing geological brain teasers. Now he's packing up his shiny silver metal briefcase with a pile of printouts of his latest findings.

He leans forward, spilling a file folder onto the floor in the process. "Portia, I was wondering if you were going to be attending the Make Palmville Beautiful Again Picnic?" He swoops down to pick up the folder with one hand but misses it by a couple of miles.

I choose to ignore the fact that he's clumsily feeling around on the floor like a blind man. Surprised by his interest in my attending the picnic, I manage, "Definitely."

"Cool." Then he turns a bright shade of crimson and backs into a nearby chair.

I pretend not to notice and look the other way, count-ing the charms on my bracelet. Behind me is a sea of eager web surfers in line, tapping their feet in unison—a rhyth-mic reminder that time is at a premium at the computer station, especially when Palmville home computers are all down. I must begin my search ASAP!

Yet this is the time that Webster, who has uttered

maybe thirty-eight words to me all year, has decided to strike up a real conversation. Of all the days and minutes that we have spent together as study partners, in line at the cafeteria, or at chance meetings on Main Street, he chooses right now to strike up a dialogue. I can't exactly explain to him the urgency behind my finger twitching and overly polite head nodding. I'll just have to fake it for a few tiny minutes more. Webster Holiday barely speaks to anyone, let alone me, so in a way, I'm kind of flattered.

He continues earnestly, "My presentation is nearly complete for the Palmville Council. Progress is slow but steady."

Now I'm tapping my foot in unison with the people in line. Through my straight pearly whites, I say, "That's just great, Webster."

He stands there without saying a word. Finally, he says quietly, "I've been meaning to tell you something."

QUESTION: What could a boy in my class with such sparkling green eyes want to tell me, Portia Avatar?

I immediately stop tapping my foot. Only one word comes out of my mouth, and it's in the form of a question. "Really?"

"It's an undisputable fact that moonquakes do occur, but they happen less frequently and have smaller magnitudes than earthquakes do on Earth."

"Is that what you wanted to tell me?"

"No, there's something else," he insists.

I gulp like a goofy dog would do in an old cartoon. "Oh?"

"There is no such thing as 'earthquake weather.' Statistically, there is an equal distribution of earthquakes in cold weather, hot weather, windy weather, and rainy weather."

Before I can say, *Webster, I really have to sign on now. My precious minutes are slipping away. It's been nice chatting with you,* he's gone, out the door in a flash. Not even so much as a good-bye.

Boys are truly perplexing creatures. I take out my PDA (which is still working) to quickly make a digital note of this undeniable fact.

I adjust my seat, determined that no matter what happens online, at least I'll make sure my offline experience is comfortable. I check the timer above the computer that tick tick ticks away. It tells me that I have eleven minutes and thirty-six seconds left out of a total of fifteen minutes. I quickly sign on to the ultimate search engine, Needle in a Haystack, to say hello to Monsieur Fate.

I find myself staring at the screen thinking of a keyword to search for my father. Nothing comes to me. I check my PDA for clues that I have gathered about him so far in the case.

List of Clues

- *Postcards from faraway places in my dreams*
- *A faded photograph of him wearing a raincoat and a hat*
- *A golden ring with unusual carvings*

 122

The clues to Patch's true identity are definitely intriguing, but they still don't offer me a clear direction. I close my eyes, trying to imagine him. The color of his eyes. His skin tone. The shape of his nose. That's when it comes to me. How entirely obvious! I'll approach my subject head-on by typing in the words "great detective." After all, Patch is the best there is, so why wouldn't someone have made note of this somewhere in the digital universe? I start counting to myself, hoping that I will find him within seconds—his name, his URL, and a link to his whereabouts.

One, two, three . . . The web page in front of me is covered with information, but nothing stands out as a clue about Patch. I do see a link to James Cagney and Great Detective Classics and another one to Great Detective Kits. I try the second link, but that just takes me to a site that sells kid costumes. On the home page there's a little boy wearing a tweed hat and a cloak. He's pretending to smoke a plastic pipe. It's totally weird. What does that costume have to do with getting to the bottom of an unsolved mystery?

It doesn't take a brain surgeon to guess that I've found

myself in a dead end digital alley. I click the back button and then continue my search. The next link that appears on top of the results page catches my eye: Great Detectives in Literature. I have a hunch there's something I can learn by following this digital trail.

Off I go, traveling the digital highway on a search for my own flesh and blood. As I wait for the super-long web page to load, my mind wanders. It occurs to me that my father must also journey on the Internet. Perhaps he has left a clue or a secret code about his location. I am fueled by this possibility and more energized than ever to uncover a new clue about him.

After a monster wait a Mount Everest–size list of web addresses appears on the screen. All the URLs link to one man. A great detective. In every image I find of him, he wears a hat and a cloak. He's smoking a curvy pipe, and he carries an oversized magnifying glass. I am most interested in his hat. It doesn't matter if it's a sketch of him or a photograph of him, it's always the same hat. This great literary detective is Sherlock Holmes. He is the most brilliant detective of all time. At least that's what they say about him on the Internet. Even though I've heard of S.

Holmes before, I really don't know that much about him. So I decide to check out his online bio.

As I dig a little deeper, I am amazed at S. Holmes's self-confidence. He claims that he can solve a mystery without ever leaving his house. How is that even halfway possible? And I keep thinking about that hat. Soon I discover that it's a deerstalker hat, used for hunting and made of twill. The twill works as camouflage so the huntees won't spot him in the woods. As if a grown man wearing a hat, a cloak, smoking a pipe, and carrying a giant magnifying glass wouldn't be seen by an animal whose main talent is sensing danger. Anyway, the hat has two brims and two side flaps, and I know for a fact that I wouldn't be caught dead wearing it. Neither would Patch! Besides, this hat was worn by a fictional character. No nonfictional human would ever consider purchasing a ridiculous hat like that.

I look at the digital clock and panic when I realize I have wasted my precious search time investigating a fake detective who wears an unattractive hat. This winding and twisting highway is turning into a dark tunnel of wrong turns. I am not making any progress whatsoever.

My attempts at finding my missing father have led nowhere.

Suddenly, it's sparkly clear to me. Of course! Patch is so entirely clever that he has even evaded the most digitally deep caverns of the World Wide Web. This is only further proof that he is the coolest, most elusive detective in the observable world.

Chapter 17

As I enter The Tent, I rehearse a pocketful of excuses for why I'm late:

1. Trash and Treasures was a radical mess, and I got so involved in my civic duty, I lost all track of time.

2. I twisted my ankle on the way home, and it's killing me!

3. I ran into Amy on the way back from Trash and Treasures, and she talked both my ears off.

I figure that Indigo will buy any one or all three of these little tales, but the good news is that I don't have to use any of them because as I scan The Tent, she's nowhere to be found.

Hap is there, cleaning off the lunch counter with a special nontoxic lemon spray. I can tell that he's got a lot on his mind by the way he furrows his brow. And his eyes are transfixed by the shiny counter. He just stares and stares at nothing. He's so absorbed in his own thoughts, he doesn't notice me enter The Tent.

I see a worn, leather-bound notebook resting on the counter. It's opened to practically the last page. I pick it up, then say casually, "Hey, Hap, is this yours?"

Startled, he reaches for it with more intensity than I've ever seen in Hap. "Yes, it's part of my latest poetry series."

I hand it to him and ask coyly, "Really?"

Hap replies in a super-serious tone, "I'm trying to decipher the concealed and metaphysical meanings of love and determine to what extent it plays a role in man's existence."

"Wow, that sounds romantic." Looking around the

restaurant past the Chinese lampshades and Tibetan wall hangings that are now covered with white plaster specks, I ask, "Have you seen Indigo?"

"She stepped out to the post office. Is there anything I can help you with?"

Relieved that the post office is open again, a sign that life might be slowly getting back to normal, I let out an exaggerated sigh. "Well, it's really a mother-and-daughter thing . . . although, actually, I was wondering something."

"Sure, what is it?"

"Do you have a father?"

I can tell that Hap is surprised by my line of questioning because he fumbles with his words. "Oh, yeah, my old man is a trip."

"He's on a trip too?"

"No, he's just this quiet character who has lived in the same small town that his parents and grandparents lived in for hundreds of years before him. He has never taken an airplane, a train, or a bus. I'm lucky if I can get him to take a walk with me around the block when I go home for Christmas."

"Interesting. Do you miss him?"

"Sometimes, but just knowing that he's happy and doing his thing is okay with me. We don't really have a lot in common. He's somewhat miffed by my current life goal of becoming a poet."

Hap's mood and expression shift suddenly. I think I have upset him by bringing up the subject of his father, but really it's because Indigo has just stepped through the beaded entrance. She is exceptionally cheery considering that her restaurant is still a total wreck. She's all bright-eyed when she says to me excitedly, "You're back!"

Hap tips his head down and returns to scrubbing the counter, looking conspicuously efficient and hardworking while occasionally trying to catch a glimpse of Indigo whenever he can steal one.

NOTE: In talking to Hap, it appears that there is a wide assortment of father types.

QUESTIONS: What type of father would Patch be? What is his exact type?

Indigo asks me all about my visit to Vera's. She loves my new hat and is more than a little bit pleased that my day of community service was so productive. When I tell her that I'm going back tomorrow, she's beyond thrilled. The best part is that I don't have to create a fictional tale about where I was today. My story about putting in community service time at Vera's definitely checks out.

3:48 P.M.,

DOWNTOWN PALMVILLE

On the way home our hybrid crawls down the streets of Palmville, which are still packed with emergency vehicles and dump trucks cleaning up the trail of earthquake mess. I notice that there are new patches of cement where the sidewalks had cracked that are still drying. A fire engine rushes by, and behind it is a fast-moving police car. The high-pitched duet makes for very tense background music. I open the car window just to test the air. My shoulders tighten when I smell the aroma of uprooted cement mixed with split wood and smoldering fire.

Just for a minute I forget that I'm on the case of a life-time. I look over at Indigo. I pretend that it's an ordinary day, just coming home from The Tent. She asks me about school and then tells me about a new recipe she's trying out, wondering if it will work or not. I pray really hard that I won't have to taste it, but of course it will appear on my dinner plate, my breakfast plate, as a midnight snack, a late-afternoon treat . . .

The fiction I create in my mind doesn't last long, for suddenly (and quietly), I panic. Tonight I will discover the truth about Patch. I make eye contact with Indigo and plant an innocent smile on my face as my left hand desperately searches my pocket for the ring. I finally feel it, then keep it buried inside my pocket for later, when Indigo will reveal the true significance of this golden band. Before the end of dinner, in less than three and a half hours, I will confront Indigo with this material evidence that links her, my dad, and me together as one complete family—bonded by pure and unconditional love.

Chapter 18

7:05 P.M.,

AVATAR KITCHEN

After another cold dinner lit by warm candlelight, I listen to Indigo go on and on about Rock. As I chew on a mouthful of sprouts, I long for comfort food. But all Indigo has to offer is lukewarm beet salad with fresh fennel topped with an overabundance of sprouts. Why not a bag of potato chips followed by a peanut butter cookie topped with a handful of chocolate mints? We've just been struck by a natural disaster. There's got to be some leeway in food consumption at the Avatars'. I'm ready to comment on this indisputable fact, but Indigo is talking at such breakneck speed, I find it hard to interrupt her.

She's gushing about how Palmville's one-and-only hero has outlined big plans to raise funds for a renovation at The Tent. Then she adds, "Thanks, Portia, you are such a wonder to me. This has been a trying time for both of us, and you've just been a dream throughout it all."

I pretend to listen to her by staring into her eyes. "Mom, I'm psyched that there's a future for The Tent."

"Rock is going to be a real friend to us."

"Us?"

"Yes. He's very fond of you."

Doubt fills my veins. How could Rock even pretend to know me? Calmly, I respond, "He's hardly spent any time with me."

"He's got good instincts and he's extremely helpful. He reminds me of an old friend of mine who once helped me out when I really needed an extra dosage of kindness." Then she takes a deep breath and smiles, most likely recalling this "old friend" of hers.

FACT: Now she's got me interested. The way she nonchalantly mentioned her "old friend" is highly suspect.

 134

My detective genes are now on full alert. "What 'old friend' are you referring to, Mom?"

My question leads Indigo to choke on a rice cracker. After she sips on a glass of filtered water, she declares that it's been a long day and it's time for bed. How entirely convenient of her to choke at such a crucial and potentially revealing moment.

Tapping my right foot to a not-so-happy beat, I am convinced that she's avoiding the subject—again! I refuse to let this latest opportunity to uncover the truth about Patch slip away from me. "Dinner is over? How is that even possible? We haven't had dessert yet. A meal is not complete without something sweet." I say this with a plastic grin on my face.

"I'm very tired, P. There are some Lemon Soy Supremes left in the dessert cabinet. One of those should do the trick."

"Mom, my mood is not even close to lemon soy."

Giant pause. I continue. "I've been wanting to tell you—"

Indigo cuts me off (very un-Indigo-like). "What is it? You can tell me anything, sweet P."

"Anything?"

Indigo nods cautiously. "You know that."

I take a breath, disguising the fact that I am bursting with close-to-impossible-to-contain nervosity. "Sometimes I just can't take this sugarless, natural grain existence. I mean, one chocolate mocha marshmallow bar with caramel cream filling isn't exactly going to destroy my future. Why is it that I can't have a normal meal like normal kids? Meatballs and french fries and frozen dinners. Besides, it's not just me. Frederick pretty much thinks that your Barley Delights are more than a little bit disgusting. In fact, he hates them!" I'm not sure why I'm telling her this when my plan was to ask her about Patch, but an emotional well has sprung and I can't stop myself. I look down at the wobbly worn floorboards. "And this house!"

Indigo utters, "The house, too?"

"It's entirely crooked, and that was before the earth-quake!"

Indigo just stares, then she speaks. "Y-you don't like my cooking?"

I slowly calm myself down and manage, "I think your certified organic banana nut bread totally rates. But truthfully, your food is a bit extreme, Mom."

Indigo's voice is shaky now. "Why didn't you tell me this sooner? It's been—"

Now it's me who cuts her off. "Eleven and a half years. Ever since I started on solids. I guess I thought you'd get upset." I look at Indigo's face, which is tensing up like a tightrope walker's middle toes. "Like you are right now." My voice unexpectedly cracks when I say this. I look at both of my hands. They're trembling.

Indigo says softly, "I want you to be healthy . . . and happy." Then hesitatingly, "My food is a part of who I am."

"You're not the only one who lives here. Don't Frederick and I have a vote on anything?"

Silence.

I check to feel if the new hat Vera gave me is still on my head. It's there! I adjust it with both hands (that are still shaking) and gather more strength. "It's not just the lack of taste sensations at home or the lopsided roof over

 137

our heads. It's everything, Mom. This is serious. The earthquake, The Tent, Frederick, your 'old friend.'"

Indigo looks at me and starts to cry. She covers up this fact by reverting to coughing on another piece of puffed rice. Then she holds out her arms to me. I find myself slowly melting into them.

I try hard not to let her tears affect me, but they do. I see that her eyes are closed, so I close mine too, imagining what she's seeing right now. It's an image of herself when she had that short haircut. It's the look in Patch's eyes whenever they were together. It's me when I was born and she held me in her arms for the first time.

Maybe Indigo is right. Maybe she is really tired. It has been an unnaturally long day.

8:12 P.M.,
MY BEDROOM

I'm on my bed checking the batteries on my PDA. There's still some juice left, so I decide to risk it. I want the Amester's thoughts on my intense conversation with Indigo. I text her my SOS message.

She writes back immediately, offering her not-so-humble opinion.

> For what it's worth, I think it's great you
> aired out your true feelings. All moms need
> reality checks once in a while. BTW, I'm so
> sure the "old friend" your mom "casually"
> mentioned at supper is totally Patch, your
> nowhere-to-be-found father. =^D Here's y:
> Whenever my cousin, Livia, talks about a
> guy she really likes who didn't work out as
> a boyfriend, she refers to him as her
> "friend." :-) She pretends he is only a
> "friend" and not an X-BF to avoid any sticky
> emotion and prevent an embarrassing display
> of waterworks. BTW, have you decided on
> what idea you'll be presenting to the Palmville
> Council? My originality is getting the best of
> me and I still can't pick one. There are too
> many astounding concepts I want to
> share with the world! I feel like I would be

depriving Palmville if I presented just one.

B4N. Me, Me, Me. :-)

Amy has confirmed my hunch about Indigo's "old friend." I input my new insights into my PDA, racing against the red warning light that blinks steadily like a lonely New England lighthouse. I quickly turn it off and give it a rest for the night. Maybe tomorrow will bring electricity and new opportunities to make my family whole again. I hope that I have not jeopardized the case with my true confessions to Indigo about life at the Avatar home according to me.

In approximately thirteen hours, I'll attempt to show Indigo the ring—again. That's not that far away, considering I've been waiting my entire infancy, toddler years, and youth to uncover the truth about my missing father.

I crawl under the bed with Frederick. He hears all about my radically eventful day in living color and in great detail, including the progress on the case. He listens carefully as I share with him how much conversational time this firefighter guy is taking up lately in our household and how I finally told Indigo that he totally despises Barley Delights. He shakes out his ears after he hears that. Then I find myself drifting to sleep to Frederick's soft purring, which sounds a lot like a lullaby.

MIDDLE OF THE NIGHT, MY BEDROOM, A DREAM

I am on a ship bigger than any I have ever seen. There is a great storm in progress. I sit below deck shivering, praying for a miracle. There is a man above me manipulating the sails, keeping the boat from capsizing. I hear his bootsteps scrambling about the upper deck. He shouts at the sky like Odysseus arguing with Poseidon on his long voyage home. Could this brave sailor be Patch? A golden butterfly flutters around me. Is it lost, or is it on its way home? DREAM ENDS.

I wake from this stormy dream and slither out from under the bed. I reach for *The Absolute Complete Unabridged Version of the History of the World* to check that my dad's

141

photograph is still there. It is. I gently kiss it while I silently make a wish for his safe return.

I look out my window. It's dawn. I can still catch the sunrise, so I rush out to the front yard. I look up at the sky, knowing that soon I'll no longer have to wonder where Patch is anymore. Both shoulders slowly sink down at the thought of having the whole family sitting together around the dinner table.

Under the rising sun I begin my preparations for this main event. I imagine what I will see when my father finally walks up the path to my house through the front door:

1. *Patch will be tall.*

2. *Patch will be smiling.*

3. *He'll be wearing a hat.*

4. *In one hand he will be carrying a suitcase. Inside the suitcase there will be souvenirs from his travels. They will not be the kind you buy at stores, but instead mementos from ancient temples, red and black seas, and rare untelevised ceremonies. These gifts will be for me.*

5. *In the other hand Patch will be carrying the most beautiful bouquet of flowers I've ever seen. These particular forms of flora cannot be found in Palmville. They will be for Indigo.*

Chapter 19

I sit down at the breakfast table to an unfamiliar sight. Indigo calls them Chocolate Coconut Confessions. I cautiously bite into one of these enticing breakfast treats that she whipped up this morning without a working stove or refrigerator. My taste buds are completely wigging out. My head spins with utter confusion. "This isn't carob, Indigo. This is totally real chocolate!"

Casually, she responds, "I remembered that I had a sample bag of chocolate shavings from one of my vendors."

I rush over to Indigo and give her a supersize grizzly bear hug. "Thanks!"

Indigo smiles. Then she hands me a bowl of something very mysterious. "This is for Frederick." I look at Indigo with a curious stare. She proudly offers, "I'm calling it Tuna on the Half Shell. No barley, I promise."

Enthusiastically, I blurt out, "That's so cool of you!"

Chocolate Coconut Confessions

INGREDIENTS:

1 1/4 cups chocolate shavings or miniature chocolate chips

1 cup sliced almonds

Pinch sea salt

1/3 cup unhydrogenated shortening (for example, any vegetable palm oil shortening that you can find at your local health food store)

1 1/4 cups sifted powdered sugar, more if needed

1 1/2 teaspoons pure vanilla

1 cup ground coconut, for rolling

DIRECTIONS:

1. Grind the chocolate shavings or miniature chocolate chips, sliced almonds, and salt in a food processor for several minutes, until powdery.

2. Remove and reserve 4 tablespoons of the mixture. Add the unhydrogenated shortening to the ground mixture and continue to blend. Slowly mix in powdered sugar and add vanilla through the feed tube. Mixture should pull together into a pliable ball, ever so slightly moist so the coconut mixture will stick to it. (Add a few more tablespoons of powdered sugar if it is too runny. Alternately, if it is too dry, add a few tablespoons of water.)

3. Stop and scrape the sides as you go, to ensure even mixing.

TO FORM AND ROLL:

1. Scoop and roll the truffle mixture into walnut-size balls, about 1 1/4 inches in diameter.

2. Toss the reserved chocolate chip and almond mixture with the cup of coconut and place in a

small bowl. Roll and press the truffles in the bowl, pressing gently yet firmly to ensure they are evenly coated.

3. Place the finished truffles on a platter or sheet pan and allow to sit for a few minutes. Store at room temperature for several days or freeze for longer periods of time and allow to sit at room temperature for an hour before serving.

Makes about three dozen

Chocolate Coconut Confessions

Halfway through my second Chocolate Coconut Confession, the Dream Checker requests a morning report. Since our big talk last night led to a miraculously sugary breakfast this morning, I am growing more confident that my case is heading toward a breakthrough too. So I boldly state without a milliliter of hesitation, "He's coming! I know it for sure this time!"

As I begin to report my dream, I notice that Indigo's face looks extra tired this a.m. I wonder how early she woke up to prepare the delicious confections? She lets out a significant sigh. But that doesn't stop me. I continue with my morning report. "Your 'friend,' my father, Patch—I dreamed it last night!"

"Portia, you've had a hard time with the earthquake and all the uncertainty."

"Why won't you just tell me what you know about Patch?"

Indigo's eyes fill with salty water like last night, only this time she speaks. "I'm only trying to protect you."

QUESTIONS: Why is it that Indigo is so secretive about the story of my conception? Why does she pretend to know so little about Patch, the father of her only child? Does she feel the loss of a husband the way I feel the loss of a father?

IDENTIFYING DATA

SUBJECT: Indigo Avatar. Thirty-seven years old. Single bohemian mother, chronically concerned about daughter's well-being. Master chef and baker. Founder of health food restaurant known as Contentment. (Note: Contentment is cur-

 148

rently under construction but promises a miraculous return.) Chronically avoids makeup. Always wears comfortable, loose-fitting long skirts that flow in the wind. Has long brown hair that's usually worn in a bun. Enjoys herbal teas and inventing recipes.

NATURE OF CONTACT: Spent nine months in subject's womb and have been raised and nurtured by subject ever since.

BACKGROUND MATERIAL: History of avoiding conflict. Does not respond easily to probing questions about the long-lost father to her only child. Is currently "just friends" with a firefighter. Recently exhibits signs that she might be open to bending her rigid food rules at home.

DIAGNOSTIC FORMULATION: Wishes to overprotect female offspring for reasons still to be determined.

DIAGNOSTIC CATEGORY: Closedmouthed Mother Syndrome.

NEXT LINE OF ACTION: Confront subject with hard evidence about Patch's identity and true nature of their relationship.

OPERATION: Prepare to hear the complete unabridged story of my life!

Just as I am about to confront Indigo with the golden band, Hap knocks at the door, signaling that our very important discussion will have to be continued in the near future. This tête-à-tête with Indigo has not exactly clarified matters. And I didn't have an opportunity to present the latest evidence of my father's existence!

8:43 A.M.,

AVATAR BACKYARD

*A*s I settle into an old lawn chair at the edge of our garden to wait for Hap and Indigo to finish plotting their day at The Tent, my eyes travel to the lemons, limes, and oranges that hang precariously from our old, worn-out trees. I look at the basil and sage growing alongside a neighboring rosemary bush so fragrant that it almost overtakes the ominous smell of smoke coming from a not-so-distant location.

Then my eyes take me to the sky. I try to piece together the messages sent to me in my dreams. Clues and symbols about my traveling father. If Indigo is right,

150

and dreams can teach us about ourselves, what is my lesson?

> **QUESTIONS:** Why does my search seem so difficult, and why is it taking so long to find my father? Why won't Indigo take my search seriously?

Of all the postcards that have come to me in my dreams, the one in which Patch told me to think of him with every sunrise stands out most in my mind. I look up at the bright, hot, California sun and squint my eyes, trying to picture him. Through my eyelashes, an image starts to slowly come into focus.

Indigo shouts from the back screen door, "We're ready!"

I'm shaken back to reality. "Okay, Mom, but first I want to check on Frederick's current state of well-being."

"Hurry, today is going to be a big day."

Indigo's words are prophetic. My highly attuned detective instincts tell me with 115 percent certainty that this will be the day when the truth of my missing father will finally be revealed.

Chapter 20

I surprise Frederick this morning by sliding a bowl of Tuna on the Half Shell under the bed. Soon he peeks his head out. I tiptoe over to him with the hope of extracting him from his hiding place. But his stealthiness eludes my clutches. For now he has chosen to remain in darkness for another day. At least I know he'll have a tasty meal, even if he has chosen to eat it alone.

I adjust my new cabbie hat in the mirror, trying out different angles. I finally settle on tilting it down to the left, just over my eye. Then I remember the photograph. I quickly slide it out of the history book and compare the way Patch wore his hat then to the way I do now. I shriek with excitement at the father/daughter parallel fashion moment!

As I head downstairs, I notice a lighter step in my walk. The heavy cloud of earthquake soot and dust is slowly lifting, and I am starting to sense that soon there will be a new beginning for the Avatar family.

I place a handful of Chocolate Coconut Confessions in a recycled paper sandwich bag. I've successfully convinced Indigo to let me ride my bike to Trash and Treasures this morning. Leftover guilt mixed with a touch of "I'm sorry for the way this morning's conversation turned out" most likely had something to do with her positive response. She hugs me good-bye, insisting that I meet her at The Tent for lunch at 12:30 p.m.

Hap sits in his battered Bug, waiting to follow Indigo to The Tent. He watches the cherry-pie-sweet mother/daughter send-off. He's got his notebook out, scribbling notes (or maybe it's poetry), turning the small graph paper pages with major-league intensity. He sees me watching him and reacts with a wink. I wink back at him, then jump on my bike and pedal off to perform another day of community service.

9:12 A.M.,

TRASH AND TREASURES

I head to Vera's shop, hoping to engage in an enlightening conversation with her. I arrive and look around the pack-rat place, past the rusted toasters, piles of dusty paperbacks, and trays of costume jewelry.

Vera is in the way back of the shop hammering a fourth leg to a beat-up coffee table. When she turns it upright, it still stands unevenly. She shouts to me, "A limping table—how much do you think it's worth, Portia?"

How did she know I was here? I hadn't even announced myself yet. She definitely has magical powers. She can read minds and tell when girl psychoanalytic detectives enter rooms without turning to look at them. "It depends on whether or not it has sentimental value to somebody."

154

"Well done! I think I'll keep it unmarked until someone shows some sentimental interest in it." Vera clears some room and places the table in full view for a potential sale. Then she turns to me. "Go ahead. You know the score."

"I'm on it, V!"

FACT: Vera believes that all once-loved objects on this earth deserve a home and that quite a few of the never-loved ones do too. She values her thousands of orphaned items that people have long ago abandoned and presides over her junkyard queendom with pride and dignity.

OBSERVATION: In my brief interaction with Vera, I have determined that she definitely has a way of seeing the invisible and hearing the inaudible.

I weave through the piles of junk and dusty countertops, trying to discover my first bit of community service for the day. I spy a pile of ancient postcards in a cracked china bowl. On inspection, I deduce that handwriting was much better in the old days. Maybe that's because those were the days before Intel chips and mouse pads. I pick one out that holds special interest. The ink is a dark purple and reminds me of the postcards that are sent to me in my dreams.

Dear Aunt Madge,

The Greeks are such treats. So warm and friendly. Now I'm off to uncover the mysteries of Egypt, and then I travel to exotic India to continue my exploration. I am so lucky to be here. And it's all because of you!

Your loving niece,
Veronica

NOTE: Maybe "Vera" is short for "Veronica"? Is there a piece of Vera Alloway's personal background that needs to be uncovered? I make a note of this for a future case.

Vera emerges, clearing her throat. She looks me up and down. "You've got something on your mind."

"Sort of." How does she know these things?

"Spill. I'm all ears." Her long silver earrings made out of decorative dessert spoons dangle gracefully against her bronze-colored, leathery skin. She moves a little closer to me, taking a seat on a torn red velvet movie seat.

"Well, I'm tired of being fatherless, so I've become a girl psychoanalytic detective with the mission of finding my missing father."

She leans forward, staring into my eyes. "I'd say that's a challenging one."

"I've had just about enough guessing. I've got to find him!"

I'm not sure what comes over me (maybe it's the hat), but I proceed to tell Vera about everything that has happened to me since the earthquake. About the blurry photograph of Patch, the recurring dreams that forecast my father's imminent return, the crazy Internet search that led me to S. Holmes and his funny hat, the troubles with Contentment, the sparkle in Indigo's eyes, the ring with the special pattern on it, the Clamdigger's unique insights, the Chocolate Coconut Confessions, my kitchen-table arguments with Indigo, and the friendly firefighter who calls himself Rock.

She takes a long, thoughtful pause. Her eyes glisten with energy. "Now, now, Portia. It sounds like this situation is teeming with mysteries and possibilities. You know, in many cultures the word 'father' has a very broad definition."

Vera pulls out an old diner stool from the clutter. She motions for me to sit on it, which I do. She continues, "There are extended families and many substitutes who play the father roles. In some cultures, when fathers go away to hunt or work for long periods of time, there are uncles, grandfathers, friends, even neighbors who offer paternal advice and guidance."

Vera then slips away into the back room. I steal a glance into the room and am shocked to see that the giant mystery object that I had seen during my last visit has grown even larger under its tarp. Vera quickly closes the door behind her. I go back to dusting and straightening.

Just before my community service is up for the day, Vera reappears from the back room, presenting me with a small, chipped clay statuette. "Portia, meet Ababinili. He's the supreme deity of the North American Chickasaw

Indians. His earthly manifestation is fire. Actually, he is the spirit of fire from the sun. The giver of warmth and light. Take him with you and let him guide you."

I hug Vera, insisting, "You're the coolest junk woman I've ever met!"

Vera nods modestly and says, "Thank you. You must continue your journey. I sense you're close."

I hold Ababinili like I am holding a diamond. He's warm, probably from bathing in the sun all day long. I am thrilled to think that Ababinili might help me solve this difficult and extremely personal case. "Vera, you are so mystically sweet." I start to leave, then turn back again. "Wait." I take off my gold-plated charm bracelet and hand it to her.

She refuses the offer, insisting that she's still got the nickel I gave her from the last trade and that's plenty enough for her. She then leans her head to the side and shoos me off. "Go now and solve the unsolvable, Ms. Avatar!"

Chapter 21

J walk my bike down the sidewalk thinking about Vera's pep talk. Then I stop to look up for a miracle in the sky. My thoughts lead me to the following conclusions:

1. *I can solve the unsolvable.*
2. *It's okay to take risks.*
3. *I must confront Indigo about Patch ASAP, and this time I won't let the opportunity slip through my fingers—no matter what happens!*

CONTENTMENT

With the mysterious carved ring in my back pocket and my Ababinili statuette tucked securely in my knapsack (right next to my PDA), I feel fully charged and ready for the "big talk." Even though I'm excited, I am also a little bit terrified, too.

QUESTIONS: What if I don't hear what I want to hear? Is it possible that Patch is not the seafaring, tanned hero with the movie-star good looks that I imagine him to be? If he's not the most elusive international detective on this side of the universe, then who is he?

Fear mixed with curiosity pushes me forward, straight through the beaded entrance of Contentment. When I step into The Tent, I spy Hap scribbling madly into his leather notebook. Next to him sits a platter of freshly prepared cashew butter and organic raspberry jam sandwiches on whole grain bread. Every few moments he takes a break, staring up at the ceiling. When he finally notices me, he smiles.

> **NOTE:** Even when Hap is smiling, his eyes look sad. Someday Hap will be the subject of one of my cases. However, this afternoon I am consumed with thoughts of sailing vessels, furious waters, hat collections, a missing father, and a gold ring.

"Hi, Hap."

"Hi, Portia. How's it going?"

Refusing to give away even half a clue about the potential turning point of my case, I answer in an exaggerated upbeat tone. "I'm doing exceptionally well. How about you?"

"I'm existing." He lightly taps his notebook cover on the counter in front of him.

My hunch is that the reason Hap is only existing and not jumping over the moon or dancing a jig is because he longs to reach out to Indigo and finally declare his love for her. But he knows that the timing isn't right for this romantic declaration, and so he keeps all his simmering emotions bottled up. I'm starting to understand why poetry was ever written in the first place. It's the bottle opener that lets out someone's innermost truths.

I decide to probe just a little. "How's your poetry going?"

Hap shrugs and blushes an unusual shade of pink. Then he taps the notebook again. "I'm working on a new poem."

"What's the subject?"

"Hard to put into words just yet." His lips quiver.

Taking his more-than-obvious clue, I back off. "Got it. Have you seen Indigo? We're supposed to have lunch together."

He stares over my shoulder, barely blinking. His eyes are fixed on The Tent's entrance. In saunter Rock and Indigo engaged in a lively conversation that mostly entails my mother giggling at everything the firefighter says and does.

Indigo rushes over to me to deliver her news. "Rock has helped secure Contentment a Palmville earthquake grant to rebuild. It's a miracle!"

"Great, Mom. I have news too. You could call it a miracle."

She tries to read my mind, but I fight her unspoken powers with a hard stare. Her voice rises at least an octave. "Is everything all right?"

For some unknown reason, I utter, "Peachy."

That's when Hap drops the platter of sandwiches on the dusty floor. Rock tries to cut the tension of the moment with his unique brand of humor. Over Indigo's forced squeaky laugh at his lame joke, Hap and I look at each other. I make sure that he sees me roll my eyes. He nods to me, then quietly retreats into the kitchen to begin preparing the lunchtime treats again.

The universe is definitely working with me (I think Ababinili has a hand in this) because just then Rock's beeper goes off. He rushes off to either rescue a kitty cat or chase after a false alarm. Indigo barely has time to say good-bye to him, and I can tell she's disappointed by that. But duty calls after all.

Now it's just Indigo and me together in the dining area—alone. I make my move. "Indigo, I'd like to talk to you."

She plays it cool. "Sure." (She stretches out the word so it sounds just like one of Frederick's purrs.)

 164

We sit down among the boxes of brown rice, cracked jars of raw honey, and spoiled cartons of vanilla soy milk. I wiggle around in my seat (which is really a crate) trying to find a comfortable spot, which might very well be impossible considering how tense this moment is right now. I blast forward. "Mom, where is he? It's important I know. I can't wait until I'm sixteen to hear all the facts."

This time Indigo doesn't even pretend not to know the subject of my inquiry. "You just need to look at yourself and you'll see him. He's right there. He's a part of you."

I am in shock at her response, but adrenaline pushes me onward. "Who?"

"Why, Patch, of course!"

I try to uncover her innermost truth by looking straight into her eyes. This is the first time I have ever heard her utter my father's name. The fact that she has said P-A-T-C-H makes him feel that much more real to me. He does exist! Indigo used his name in a complete sentence.

Long, dramatic pause.

During this pause I try to catch my breath, which seems to have escaped me. I look at Indigo suspiciously. "Really? Which part?"

Indigo smiles softly. "That's for you to discover."

IMPORTANT FACT: Indigo is cleverly avoiding the subject (again!), but at least she has offered me a clue.

I continue my line of questioning. "Do you mean it might be one of those unsolvable mysteries?"

She takes her time as she replies. "Well, I think that it would be true to say that it's not solvable right now. No one ever knows the future."

This crucial moment is supposed to be loud, boisterous, and monumental. Timpanis, trumpets, and screeching violins should be filling the airwaves right about now. But instead, it's quiet and still. Strangely serene.

Indigo looks and speaks with such convincing calm. It's like she's been planning this moment for a long, long time. Just like I have. I slowly take out the carved ring from my pocket and look into her eyes as I boldly ask, "Then what's this?" I hand her the golden band.

Now it's Indigo who's shocked. No words, just more silence. After minutes pass like long hours, she asks, "Where did you find this?"

I tell her about the folder marked CONFIDENTIAL and how the ring must have fallen out of its hiding spot with the force of the earthquake.

> **NOTE:** My story isn't exactly nonfiction, but I'm covering my bases just in case Indigo's present state of mind has taken a turn away from calm, cool, and collected.

We just sit there like mannequins at a tea party.

> **IMPORTANT NOTE:** Silence can be a pretty powerful state between two people.

Indigo places the ring in the palm of my hand. She tells me gently, "It's yours."

"Mine? That's impossible! This is your wedding

ring—material evidence of the indestructible love between you and Patch!"

A bright red color slowly covers Indigo's stunned face. "You're right."

"I knew it!"

I'm now entirely on target and closer than ever to breaking the case of my missing father! My head spins, but I'm ready to hear the truth. My hands are now grasping the edge of my seat so there's no way I can fall off the crate.

Indigo explains, "This is a wedding ring, but it's not mine."

The meaning of what Indigo has just said is opera-singer loud and clear. My hunch was wrong, and I have turned up another dark alley. I whisper to myself, "This can't be true, this can't be true!" And for one split second I wonder how S. Holmes would handle a setback like this one. Even though he's a piece of fiction and another person's invention, he does seem pretty smart. Would he give up, or would he find the inner strength to keep going?

Indigo continues calmly, "This was your great-grand-mother's ring. It's been in the family for generations."

I finally speak. "Are you sure?"

"Absolutely. And now it's yours."

"What do I do with it?"

"Keep it in a safe place. In time you'll be able to answer that question."

There she goes dropping hints again!

I put on the ring and turn it around and around on my finger, trying to figure out just how much older I'll have to be until it fits me perfectly. My thoughts drift back to the case. I look into Indigo's eyes and take a risk. "Does this mean there wasn't a love connection between you and Patch?"

Indigo is officially overwhelmed. I can tell because the red color in her face still has not faded. "You were born with love all around you." She hugs me so hard, I can barely breathe. But I pretend I'm breathing just fine since I know this is one of those turning points you see near the end of a full-length dramatic movie. She comes out of our embrace, looks at me, and says, "I love you more than anything in the world."

I've traveled this far in my search, and I'm so close, but still no Patch. Indigo is telling me everything I already

know, not what I want to know. I have the assurance that I was indeed a welcome arrival to planet Earth by one of my parents, but what about the other one?

It's not a gigantic surprise that Indigo loves me—the way she cares about me every day, how she feeds me and does backflips to make me happy. Now she's even starting to change the menu at home for me. So why not really make me happy by telling me what I need to know about Patch?

I try to open my mouth to tell her this, but my two arms open instead. I reach out to the one person who has looked after me since I let out my first cry. My one and only mother.

IMPORTANT NOTE: In life we are born to one mother. Although it's easy to imagine life without a father (I've been living that way for twelve years), I can't imagine what my days in this world would even look like without Indigo there to share them with me.

In a hurry to get my words out, I rush through each syllable. "I love you, Mom!"

Just then the electricity stutters back on. Lights blink from overhead. All the mechanical things in the restaurant start to cough, overtaking the silence with loud, clunky, whirring sounds.

Hap shouts to Indigo that he needs her in the kitchen right away. Duty calls, so she makes her escape. I can tell that when she leaves the scene this time, there's more she wants to say to me, but for some reason, she stops short.

QUESTIONS: What is Indigo's innermost truth that she holds on to so tightly? Will I ever know the true untold story of my father?

Chapter 22

The sun fades over the pink and purple sky. Back at home now, I crawl up to my room, exhausted from all of today's developments.

As soon as I enter my room, I notice a suspicious lump sticking up from under my sheets. There, sleeping on my unmade bed with his furry head resting cozily on my feather pillow, is Frederick! He opens his eyes slowly, still in sleep mode, taking his time, stretching his long body as far as it will go, and then he finally greets me. He casually slips out from under the covers, pretending that he had never been frightened by the earthquake in the first place. I choose to play along. I'm just happy to see my little cat out in the open. I pick him up, and he immediately licks my face puppy-style. "I missed you so much, Frederick. Welcome back to the real world. You've got to hear the latest about the case."

Frederick jumps out of my arms and starts running around in perfect circles. Is Frederick just happy to be out from under his dark cloud of fear, or is he telling me something? Last time Frederick ran around in perfect circles, the earthquake hit Palmville.

I kneel down to get on Frederick's level, attempting a heart-to-heart, but he's too frisky for a summit meeting about predicting earthquakes. He runs away, wagging his tail, sniffing the other side of the room, searching for something extremely important.

For now I wipe the thought of experiencing another earthquake out of my mind. Instead, I think about my family's past and future and how I fit into that intricate puzzle. I take the golden ring, my very first family heirloom, and place it carefully in one of my jewelry boxes that has managed to survive the earthquake.

I dig around for my hand mirror and find it buried deep under a pile of clothes on my rug. I pick it up and take a look at myself, contemplating what Indigo said about discovering the parts of myself that are like Patch.

My PDA lights up. Relieved that my connection to the world of friends is now in excellent working order, I check to see who's texting me. It's the Amester. Her dramatic timing is once again flawless.

I read her message:

> I've got it! :-D I figured out my idea for the
> picnic, and it's beyond awesome. I can't tell
> you what it is, because it's that good. Not
> that I think you'd steal it or anything, it's just
> that with intellectual property, you've got to
> be super-international-spy careful. \') Since
> we're on the subject of spies, how's your
> case going?

I respond:

> I'm totally stumped. Indigo told me
> I could find Patch if I just looked at myself.
> She claims he's a part of me. :~/

Amy replies right away:

> Hello? Have you looked in the mirror lately?
> So is Indigo. You're just like your mom. The
> mocha brown hair, the almond-shaped eyes,
> the perfect skin. Duh! You two could totally
> be sisters! :)

Since the case began, I've been thinking solely about the detective genes I inherited from my father. But what about Indigo? She's played a leading role in who I am. I only spend every day with her!

I text Amy:

> Big thanks for the mother/daughter
> comparisons, Ame! I'm not sure how yet,
> but I suspect your wisdom is going to help
> the case. You're the best friend a girl
> psychoanalytic detective could ever ask for!
> I hope you make enough cash to buy a
> mansion from your new big idea's earnings.
> ^^^ Gotta go, bye! :-D

My hands shake with excitement as I set down my PDA. I pick up the mirror and take another look. Of course—it's me!

The biggest clue of my biggest case is *me*!

If I make a list of all the parts of myself that are like Indigo and all the parts of myself that are like Patch, I can deduce what I've actually inherited from my missing father.

PLAN OF ACTION: Make a list of the qualities I possess. Attempt to solve the seemingly insolvable. Determine the identity of my missing father.

Indigo

- *Wavy brown hair*
- *Almond-shaped dark brown eyes*
- *Clear skin*
- *Asks a lot of questions*
- *Curious about people*
- *Analyzes dreams*
- *Keen observer of details*
- *Aware of her environment (with the exception of not*

picking up on Hap's lovesick state)

- *Enjoys listening to other people's stories*

Patch

-

I find myself feeling disappointed when I realize that I really don't know Patch at all, except what I dream about him. I don't know his habits or where he lives. Worst of all, I don't have a clue about what parts of me are even remotely like him.

VERY IMPORTANT QUESTIONS: What if Patch isn't a detective? Could that be the truth that Indigo has been hiding from me?

Just then my PDA lights up again. It's a call from Amy. She has already started the conversation without me. Before I have a chance to tell her about the latest major development in my case, she's halfway through three sentences of her own creation. From what I gather, she's all worked up because her oldest brother, Chester, just stole her new big idea and now she's back to being idea-less. "Portia, it's just that you are swimming in originality, and since Chester stole my get-rich-in-a-hurry-by-saving-Palmville idea, and since I'm so busy with Keithy and all the burdens that come with popularity, plus keeping up morale in Palmville during the earthquake and scoring extra points with Miss Killjoy, I don't have time to come up with another new idea."

Miraculously, Amy sneezes during the conversation (if you call her one-way talkfest a conversation), and I find my opening. I quickly tell her about my list. After I read it to her, she takes a long pause. I can almost hear her computing her thoughts in her head from over the phone waves. Then she offers, "Your mom sounds like a total detective. It's obvious that your girl psychoanalytic detective genes are inherited from Indigo, not your missing dad."

IMPORTANT QUESTION: Why is it that something that is right in front of you is the hardest thing to see?

The wind chimes ring from downstairs. I hang up with Amy.

It's time for me to take the case to a new level. I've had just about enough of Indigo's cloudy hints and hazy clues. She's bottlenecking my progress on the case. My search will not end until the whole truth about Patch is revealed. S. Holmes wouldn't give up, especially now.

QUESTION: If Patch is not an international detective, then what does he do for a living? In what part of the world does he lay his hat(s)? Where does he call home?

Chapter 23

The power is back on, so we have a warm meal for the first time in days. It's simple and not too extreme. Whole wheat pasta with organic roasted tomato sauce. All during dinner I am really quiet.

Of course Indigo Avatar notices Portia Avatar's noiseless mood. "Did you decide to stop your search?"

Perfect opening. Thanks, Indigo! "No. In fact, I think I might be making some headway." I say this to throw her offtrack.

Calmly, she says, "I see. More pasta?"

I shake my head. Then I take this opportunity to

confront Indigo about Patch. This will be it. The whole truth revealed. "What was Dad like? Was he strong? Did he have insight and wisdom?"

She gets really quiet. "Portia, we've been over this. I just want you to be happy. Now remember to save some room for dessert."

The telephone rings. Indigo uncharacteristically jumps up from her seat to grab it. Usually, telephone calls are banned during dinner, but tonight appears to be an exception.

OBSERVATION: It's almost as if Indigo was expecting a call from someone. Could that "someone" be firefighter intruder guy, Rock?

It turns out it's Amy on the line. She finally rang the home number after failing to reach me on my PDA, which I left upstairs. Relieved that our intense conversation has been interrupted, Indigo gladly hands me the phone and insists that I take the call.

Amy begins by bragging about the fact that Keithy has called her exactly seven times since we last spoke to

confirm that he's going to be her date for the picnic tomorrow. Then she switches gears abruptly, confessing that she's panicked because she still doesn't have a clue about how to make Palmville beautiful again. In the same breath she asks, "Am I crazy, or does nerd boy Holiday have a major crush on you?"

I ignore her Webster Holiday question. If I did choose to answer it, which I don't and I won't, my answer would be that Webster has definitely shown more interest in me than he ever had pre-earthquake.

NOTE: An earthquake can bring many things to the surface, maybe even Webster's potential innermost "feelings" for me. The thought of a boyfriend, even if he's just a practice one, makes me jittery. I never knew growing up would be so nerve-racking!

While Amy is still on the phone and still idea-less, she asks me what I'll be proposing to the Palmville Council. I've been so consumed with my case that I forgot about thinking up an idea. I look down at the far end of the kitchen table, which is covered with a combination of flashlights, matches, lemons, candles, aromatherapy oils, bottled water, fig bars, homemade blended hand cream, dry roasted cashews, golden raisins, and cherry pop lip gloss. I quickly deduce that Indigo and I could totally create our own Earthquake Preparedness Kit to raise money to make Palmville beautiful again.

So I tell Amy about my Earthquake Preparedness Kit concept and suggest that she look around her house for a clue of her own. The perfect idea is probably right in front of her too. She just can't see it right now.

Amy does a 360-degree turn. After she's finished rotating in a complete circle, she claims that all that's in her line of sight is her unruly collection of brothers and sisters. She looks down. "And my new pair of pink espadrilles." She sighs.

"You're going to come up with a stellar idea. I just know it!"

Indigo stares at me with that "you've been on the phone long enough" look, so I gracefully say good-bye and leave Amy to arm wrestle with her own imagination.

Indigo thinks the Avatar Earthquake Preparedness Kit is a brilliant idea. For dessert we munch on Indigo's latest creations: freshly baked Strawberry Security

Squares. She carefully watches me as I bite into one. With my mouth still full, I say, "It's really good, Indigo."

"Is it sweet enough?"

"Honestly, it could be sweeter. And maybe a little more crunchy."

"I'll make a note for the next time." She smiles. "Thanks for the input, P."

> **NOTE:** It feels like an elephant has been airlifted off my shoulders now that I can comfortably tell Indigo how I really feel about her food creations. Maybe together we can come up with super-fantastic taste sensations for the reopening of Contentment.

Strawberry Security Squares

INGREDIENTS:

1 1/2 cups old-fashioned oats

1 cup all-purpose flour

2/3 cup brown sugar, packed

1/2 teaspoon baking soda

1/2 teaspoon salt

8 tablespoons butter, melted

1 1/2 cups strawberry jam

Zest of one lemon

Butter or nonstick cooking spray

DIRECTIONS:

1. Preheat oven to 350°.

2. Mix together oats, flour, brown sugar, baking soda, and salt. Using a wooden spoon, stir in the melted butter. Place two-thirds of the mixture in a buttered baking pan (or one sprayed with nonstick cooking spray) and pack down firmly with fingers.

3. Stir together the strawberry jam and lemon zest. Spread evenly over the packed crust and sprinkle the remaining oat mixture over the top. Bake for 30 to 35 minutes, until the crust is a deep brown and the filling has bubbled through on the sides.

4. Cool for at least an hour and serve

Makes about 12 squares

As for the emergency kit, it includes only the most essential stuff you need when an earthquake strikes:

1. **CHERRY POP LIP GLOSS:** *When you are caught in an earthquake, ninety-nine times out of a hundred, it's a surprise. It's very possible that you will have to see all your neighbors and several emergency workers, so a little lip gloss will come in handy. Not to mention that it gets very dry and dusty after an earthquake, and lip gloss will help in that department too.*

2. **TALL BOTTLE OF CRYSTAL CLEAR FILTERED WATER:** *This is most necessary to quench the thirst and the soul.*

3. **VIAL OF SOOTHING LAVENDER OIL:** *According to Indigo, if you rub just a drop or two on your temples, you can handle just about anything since lavender calms the nerves.*

4. TUBE OF SWEET ORANGE-SCENTED HOME-MADE HAND CREAM: *This is useful if you have to sit outside waiting for the emergency vehicles to check out your house for electrical damage and gas leakage. No matter what's going on around you, at least your hands will be smooth and smell delicious.*

5. FLASHLIGHT: *In case the shaking happens at night.*

6. A DOZEN FIG BARS AND A BAG OF GOLDEN RAISINS AND CASHEWS: *Clearly, you'll need sustenance (if possible, include a chocolate bar as well).*

7. TIN OF TUNA ON THE HALF SHELL: *Use this to lure your cat out of whatever hole he has decided to hide in, ensuring a complete and happy family circle. (Note: The type of food can be modified to suit your pet.)*

J take a refreshing rose blossom shower. It's my first shower since the earthquake, which makes it extra refreshing. Then I slip under my warm bedcovers. Frederick is already there, fast asleep, content that the earth isn't moving anymore. I hear the phone ring from downstairs. I can tell from the muffled giggles and occasional high-pitched laughter that it must be Rock pouring on his charm once again. Indigo has dated men here and there over the years, but the way she looks at this firefighter guy seems different.

> **QUESTIONS:** If Indigo ever started a serious relationship with someone, would I be able to a handle a new person in my life? Am I allergic to change?

Just as I close my eyes, my computer chirps like a hungry chickadee. Who would be e-mailing me this late at night? It must be Amy in need of some more creative input. I force myself out of bed to check the message.

I'm surprised to discover that the message is not from Amy, whose e-mail address is mememe@palmville.net. It's from an address I don't recognize.

> To: pavatar@palmville.net
> From: nextstepmars@palmville.net
> I've loaded some new software into my microprocessor and I'm doing some beta testing. I thought I'd send you this e-mail to see if it's working. Did you get it? By the way, will I see you at the picnic tomorrow?
> Have a good night, Miss Avatar.
> Signed,
> Webster

I must be dreaming. It's from Webster. Webster Holiday has written me an e-mail? I don't even blink (or breathe). My hands start typing as fast as a professional secretary's on the top floor of a Fortune 500 company.

To: nextstepmars@palmville.net

From: pavatar@palmville.net

Hi Webster! Yes, we are definitely connected.

I mean, your e-mail is definitely connected!

How are you? See you tomorrow!!

Au revoir,

Portia

As I hit the send button, I realize that adding something in French at the end was so entirely and completely ridiculous. Webster is going to think I'm such a total dweebette. Frederick jumps on my lap, reassuring me that I'm not the loser I think I am. His purrs drown out my concerns. For now it's time to sleep off the day.

Chapter 24

$\mathcal{I}$ sit on my slanted front porch watching Frederick frolic in the overgrown grass, chasing a golden butterfly. It's dry with a dusty smell in the air. Earthquake weather. I try not to think about that fact. Powerful dry winds start to pick up. Leaves fly everywhere. Our funky mailbox at the end of the rocky path suddenly tips over. I run to try to fix it. As I secure it back into the ground, I casually look inside.

I check out the snail mail. But the mailbox is not over-flowing with postcards from a long-lost father saying that he is planning to return. Zero again. Total strikeout. A golden butterfly appears from inside (like in my past dreams) and flies away. I keep this to myself.

Just then Webster pedals by on his ten-speed. He squeaks to a halt when he sees me. "Greetings, Miss Avatar. I'll see you at the Make Palmville Beautiful Again Picnic." He looks down at his oversized watch. "It commences in approximately 3.46 hours."

"I'll be there."

"I've got to put the finishing touches on my electromagnetic wave detector from outer space and complete the flowcharts."

All I can say is "Cool."

Wind chimes shatter this minor miracle of a moment. Webster Holiday is asking me on kind of a date (I think). Indigo sticks her head out the front door. "Honey, it's time to check your dreams."

Webster has a confused expression on his face when he hears this, then pedals as fast as he can in the direction of his home with barely a good-bye. I'm majorly mortified.

Freddy Fred Frederick rushes across the yard to greet me with his tail wagging. I swear, if he could bark, that's what I would be hearing right now. Just before he reaches me, he turns about-face and suddenly starts digging up an imaginary object in the front yard. Frederick has completely missed this extra-large embarrassing exchange.

> **FACT:** Cats are often sheltered from life's harsher realities, such as mothers humiliating their innocent daughters in front of members of the opposing gender.

Frederick's extreme cuteness factor helps ease the pain only slightly.

8:26 A.M.,

AVATAR KITCHEN

*I*ndigo is dressed in a long flowered skirt and an embroidered white shirt. She looks unusually refreshed this morning. I wonder if her marathon phone conversation with the friendly firefighter last night has anything to do with her sunny mood.

 193

Seated at the table, Indigo proudly reveals a plate containing an eggplant omelet accompanied by eggplant toast.

NOTE: Indigo has decided to test out eggplant recipes for The Tent's upcoming reopening. The earthquake has provided her with a great opportunity to start fresh and design a brand-new menu.

I hesitate at first. I mean, eggplant is not exactly morning food, but I give it a try anyway. Indigo follows my every move. She looks me in the eyes. "Too extreme?"

If I am to be the official taste-tester for the new menu, I'm going to have to be honest, so I nod. "Uh-huh."

Indigo nods back, clearly anticipating my response. "Got it. I'll see what I can do about that. I made some more of those Chocolate Coconut Confessions."

"Perfection, Mom." I hold up my fresh apple-ginger juice. "Cheers." Indigo clanks her handmade mug of chamomile tea against my glass.

I bite into a Confession as Indigo begins her morning dream checking. "I can't wait to hear where you traveled last night."

"I really don't remember what I dreamed last night. Maybe I didn't dream at all."

"We all dream, sweetheart. I wonder what it means when we forget. What do you think?" Clever Indigo. She's throwing this one back at me. A psychoanalytic trick dating back to Monsieur Freud himself. Then she surprises me. Indigo looks at me with a concerned and serious expression. "I've decided to start my own search for Patch. The truth is, I have no idea where he is."

My jaw drops. I know if I looked in a mirror right now, I wouldn't recognize myself. It's the biggest breakthrough of my case, and I don't know what to say. Of all the thousands of words in the dictionary, I can't think of a single one, so I just stare at Indigo. Then, without thinking too much, I reach over and hug her. A salty tear rolls down my cheek. I try really hard not to let her see it.

Chapter 25

I count only two clouds in the sky. Indigo carefully hands me the Earthquake Preparedness Kit. But not before I adjust my cabbie hat and reapply my cherry pop lip gloss in the rearview mirror.

As we get out of our parked hybrid and walk toward the park, I notice that the whole town has rallied together to make this an extra-special day. Ben and Joe from Bits and Bytes are at one booth giving away free mocha lattes and tech support. I also spot Mr. Scuzzy chatting it up with Miss Killjoy in front of the Palmville Middle School booth, which features flyers instructing kids about how to handle an earthquake during school hours.

I wonder if there's a sparkle between them? It's hard to tell under the glaring sun above us, but that thought might be worthy of more investigation. I make a note in my PDA, which now has a fully charged battery and is back in working order.

Then I spot the Palmville Council in the process of reviewing Webster's presentation, an elaborate graph of seismic waves and flowcharts with arrows pointing in a hundred different directions. A cool Palmville breeze sweeps through the park. Webster turns to look over his shoulder and catches my eye. I wave. He nods shyly as the judges check out his proposal with great interest.

NOTE: I'm relieved that Webster doesn't think I'm a total dweebette.

I feel someone tapping on my right shoulder. It's the Clamdigger. "I told you nerd boy was crushing on you. And it seems like it's mutual. How quaint!"

"Me? I was just looking over at the judges."

"Whatever. You know, Keithy is getting me a cold drink. Keithy is such a loyal BF, I can't believe my good fortune."

"Great, Ame. Did you come up with an idea for your presentation?"

"OMG! You totally saved me last night. After we hung up, I decided that what I have to offer Palmville is my extraordinary sense of fashion and my crazy family, so we all (minus Chester) decided to chip in and paint the Community Center next Saturday. I'm going to be the key color consultant for the project. I'm thinking sea green with light peach accents."

Amy fixes her hair band and then adjusts her training bra. "That'll go on my resume for sure. Miss Killjoy won't have a choice but to give me, like, I don't know, two hundred extra points for that major good deed."

I'm glad Amy is happy with her idea. It's a win-win situation because Palmville gets a partial face-lift and Amy won't be calling me anymore for new ideas.

Just then a sweaty, pigeon-toed Keithy rushes over to Amy. He hands her a paper cup filled with warm lemonade. Amy winks at him and grabs the cup. She swigs it.

 198

Then, with a sour face, she says, "I told you extra sugar, Keithy. You know how I like things sweet!"

I conveniently slip away before a "lovers' quarrel" ensues. Indigo is holding our spot in the food line. She waves me over. As I make my way to her, I notice that Vera has arrived. She's lugging something on a wheeled cart covered in a tarp that looks conspicuously like the mysterious object she was hiding in the back room at Trash and Treasures. An impromptu crowd forms around her. She dramatically pulls off the tarp, revealing a junk sculpture made of broken objects from the quake. Vera plans to donate her latest junk masterpiece to town hall.

A burst of applause spontaneously erupts. The judges' heads turn to look at the sculpture. They break out in applause as well. Vera stands next to her prized art piece looking totally humble, but there's a major sparkle in her eyes. When she sees me, she waves enthusiastically and shouts, "It's good to see you. Will you be coming by the shop?"

I shout over to her, "Of course! I'll see you tomorrow after school!"

 199

Vera looks at me with a knowing smile. "Great. . . . Hey, Portia!"

I move a little closer. "What?"

"Love the hat!"

"Thanks!" That's when I think I see the nickel I gave Vera. It's part of her sculpture, sparkling under the sun, right on top!

FACT: Even after I finish my post-earthquake good deed of helping Vera clean up the mess in her shop, I plan on spending more time with her. She seems like a pretty cool person who could teach me a lot.

When I turn back to Indigo, I discover that Rock has appeared and has captured her total attention. I slowly approach them, feeling uncomfortable as I watch my mother giggling, wiggling, and swooning. Rock sees me coming. He waves at me. I surprise myself by waving back at him.

QUESTION: Could I possibly be getting used to this guy who has supremely intruded on my family and home?

FACT: Indigo enjoys the exchange immensely.

 200

The afternoon is a big success and so is our Earthquake Preparedness Kit. But the judges hand first prize to Hap, who presents his poem about unending love in the midst of trembling, twirling, and unpredictable life events. His eyes are on Indigo the entire time he recites it to the crowd. But she's oblivious and more interested in what Rock is thinking than what Hap is emoting. The poem is heartfelt and lifts the town's spirits. Maybe that's just what everyone needs right now.

I look around me. There are families everywhere. Most have fathers attached to them. But some are fatherless, just like mine is (at the moment). It might be that the fathers in some of the fatherless families are at work or on a business trip or at home repairing a damaged wall from the earthquake, but I bet that some of the families are coexisting without a dad at home.

I think back to what Vera said to me yesterday, remembering how she had expanded the definition of a father. It makes me think that although this temporary fatherless situation feels unique, maybe there are other kids out there in the same position as I am. To date, I haven't met any of them, but I can guess that my hunch is correct.

This substitute-father theory starts to settle in a little more. I close my eyes to make a mental list in my mind of all the father-type role models in my life:

1. Hap
2. Rock?
3. Mr. Scuzzy (total weirdage!)

QUESTIONS: What is a complete family, anyway? Have I measured my life by what I don't have instead of by what I do have?

What I Don't Have
• *A father who lives in my home with me, my mother, and my cat*

What I Do Have
• *A loving mother*
• *A loyal cat*

- *A roof over my head (even if it's crooked)*
- *Food to sustain me (even if it's on the health food side most of the time)*
- *A best friend who cares about me (despite her need to be the center of the universe 24/7)*
- *A wise junk lady who offers priceless advice when I really need it*
- *A new hat*
- *An heirloom that connects me to my family's past*
- *An Ababinili statuette to bring me good luck*
- *A sous-chef friend who will cook anything I want, as long as it's vegetarian and sugar-free*
- *A possible new boyfriend?*
- *A list of potential "substitute" father figures*

FACT: The haves way outscore the have-nots.

On the way back to the car Indigo randomly asks me to name my favorite color.

I tell her I've been thinking a lot about electric purple lately. She smiles and says, "If it's all right with you and

Frederick, I've decided to renovate the house. And your room is first!"

"For real?"

"Can I count that as a yes?"

"Totally . . . and I know I speak for Frederick too!"

"Then it's unanimous!"

While Indigo carefully steers us home, I see that Palmville is starting to get back to normal. Most of the businesses are finishing their cleanup, gearing up for tomorrow, which will be a business-as-usual Monday. I think about my room's upcoming makeover, imagining a whole new look and attitude. Paisley, stripes, flowers, electric purple, lemon-lime, mellow sage, retro chic, zoned-out Zen? Colors and patterns spin around and around. I'm officially on interior designer overload so decide to take a break—temporarily.

Chapter 26

I flip through *The Absolute Complete Unabridged Version of the History of the World* and pull out the old torn and faded picture of Patch. I place it as close to my eyes as I possibly can before it goes completely out of focus. I want to know more about this photograph!

QUESTION: Was it a parting gift that Patch left for Indigo before he disappeared into a misty dawn?

My eyes lead me to my new statuette of Ababinili, who now stands on my shelf. Something catches my eye.

It's the pattern on his clothing. It looks familiar, but I can't place why or how. I quickly reach into the jewelry box where I am storing the Avatar family heirloom and take out the golden band with the mysterious carvings. When I hold the ring up next to Ababinili, I see that the pattern on the sun god's clothing matches the carvings on my great-grandmother's ring!

> **QUESTIONS:** Did Vera know that these patterns were the same? Is that why she gave me the statuette?

Whether it's a coincidence or a sign from the heavens or the clever workings of the mystic junk lady, I'm holding on to both of these precious objects that possess great sentimental value to me.

I take the photograph of my missing father and place it under my pillow. Tomorrow I'll show it to Indigo and we'll begin our search (together this time) to find Patch.

Frederick leaps onto the bed to receive his nightly dose of chin scratches. It's lights-out. I decide to visualize solid ground. I've had enough stirring up for a while.

I slip under the covers and let my mind just wander.

Colorful, foggy images of Indigo, Amy, Frederick, Rock, Hap, and Vera pass through my mind. I think I even see Webster somewhere out there in the shadows. My mind takes me to streets lined with sky-high palm trees. There's an aromatic wireless coffeehouse, a dusty junk shop, and a homey health food restaurant called Contentment (under construction). Red, orange, and pink bougainvilleas transport me to a backyard garden overflowing with fresh fruit, vegetables, and herbs. Then I see a big blue ocean and beautiful lush canyons. Of course I'm in Palmville. My home sweet home.

3:56 A.M.,

MY BEDROOM

*I*t's early in the morning when I awake to a shaking sensation. It's an earthquake! It lasts for only a few seconds (maybe six).

I hear my concerned mother shout from her bedroom. "Portia, are you okay? We just had an earthquake!"

I see that Frederick is buried under the covers and

hasn't retreated to his not-so-secret hiding place. Grabbing Frederick and holding on tight, I shout back to Indigo, "Frederick and I are both fine."

Indigo rushes into my dark room and gives me a warm hug. "I love you. You don't know how precious you are to me."

4:10 A.M.,
AVATAR BACKYARD

*I*ndigo decides to shrug the whole earthquake thing off for the night. She breaks open the Earthquake Preparedness Kit prototype instead. We sit on the back stoop, looking at all the sparkling stars that fill the sky. The smell of stirred-up dust once again fills the air. Frederick jumps on my lap, purring up a storm.

We all look at the same expansive sky, but we are caught in our separate thoughts. Indigo thinks about the renovation at The Tent and wonders how eggplant caviar would go over as a new lunch special. I think she also wonders what post-earthquake rescue Rock is leading right now in Palmville. Meanwhile, Frederick stares at a nearby tree and thinks about what he would do if he ever actually caught a squirrel. I stare at the luminous full moon and think about the new look for my room. Then I picture Patch, my long-lost father, on a boat riding the current. Since he is probably on the exact opposite side of the world, he's waking up right now, drinking water from a cup he has just dipped into the blue sea that surrounds him for miles and miles. The salty, foreign taste in his mouth reminds him that he is far away from home.

QUESTION: Even with Indigo's help, I wonder if I will ever find the subject of the most important case of my career— Patch?

The world is a big place filled with unexpected occurrences like earthquakes and maybe even someday the return of a missing father from a certain unknown geographic location. I think that I won't have to wait until I'm sixteen now to discover the truth about Patch. If Indigo's search goes well, I could hear about his whereabouts within weeks or even days. The thought of knowing that my father has an address somewhere on this planet sends chills through my body.

The Case of Patch, My Missing Father: A Man of Many Hats is not officially closed. To date, the findings are inconclusive.

5:03 A.M.,

MY BEDROOM

I stare up at the dark ceiling. A single bird chirps loudly outside my window. Another feathered friend accompanies him from a nearby tree. The singing continues, and I think about how cool it is of Indigo to start her search for Patch. I can tell this will be difficult for her, but what I gather from our talks over the past few days is that she has finally discovered that her loving and attentive daughter (me) would much prefer that she address the Patch situation openly, rather than avoid the subject and pretend not to care. I wonder what other unexpected mother/daughter breakthroughs we'll experience as we set sail on our journey together to find Patch.

The birds outside my window continue their duet as I close my eyes and sink deep into my pillow.

I look forward to dreaming.

Summer Camp Secrets

One Summer.
One Sleepaway camp.
Three thrilling stories!

How far will Kelly go to hold on to her new friends?

What happens when Judith Ducksworth decides to become J.D. at camp?

Can Darcy and Nicole's friendship survive the summer?